STRANGE LIGHTS
IN A
DARK WORLD

AN OLD WORLD SAGA NOVELLA

STRANGE LIGHTS IN A DARK WORLD

First edition published June 2023.

Book cover art by warrendesign
Manuscript design by Joel Preston

ISBN 978-0-6454676-9-7 (Paperback)
ISBN 978-0-6457791-0-3 (eBook)

To contact the author email: contact@joelprestonauthor.com
joelprestonauthor.com

STRANGE LIGHTS
IN A
DARK WORLD

AN OLD WORLD SAGA NOVELLA

JOEL PRESTON

Other Novels by This Author:

In the Shadow of Monstrous Things

Rise Golden Apollo

In the Shadow of The Old World

Fall Silver Artemis

Novellas by This Author:

The Wendigo Incident: An Old World Saga Novelette

Earth's Mightiest Warrior: An Old World Saga Novella

This novella is dedicated to Jan and Petra Berghuis, who taught me to always embrace new ideas, no matter how bizzare.

IN READING ORDER

This novella takes place **between** *The Old World Saga Book Four:*
Fall Silver Artemis and *The Old World Saga Book Five:* **In the
Shadow of the Sundered King.**

*For maximum enjoyment of this novella it is best to have read the entire saga in the
order displayed below prior to commencing.*

1.  IN THE SHADOW OF
MONSTROUS THINGS

2.  RISE GOLDEN APOLLO

3.  FEAR THE FULL MOON
(coming soon)

4.  THE WENDIGO INCIDENT

5.  IN THE SHADOW OF
THE OLD WORLD

6.  EARTH'S MIGHTIEST WARRIOR

7.  FALL SILVER ARTEMIS

8.  STRANGE LIGHTS IN A
DARK WORLD

9. IN THE SHADOW OF
THE SUNDERED KING
(coming soon)

CHAPTER 1

THE DISAPPEARANCE OF
RANDALL DARE

- FEBRUARY 2 2021 -
DUNEDIN, NEW ZEALAND

In a particularly unremarkable classroom stood a remarkable man. Well, he'd been told his whole life that he was remarkable, though he didn't feel all that special. His name was Randall Dare and he'd always hated his name. It was old-school and dorky. Nothing irked him more than when people would call him *Randy* in a juvenile attempt to belittle. Something that had, as recently as last year, happened quite frequently.

Randall paced back and forth in front of a blackboard impressively laden with complex symbols and numbers. His brow was furrowed with concentration, yet he couldn't stop his mind wandering from the task at hand. He was caught in a bizarre jumble of memories of the past and confusion about the present. It was as if his mind had been thrown into a perpetually spinning washing machine, with the same ideas bouncing up and down, over and over, slowly driving him mad.

Madness was a good word for his life right now.

Randall had recently found himself in the most peculiar of circumstances. Here he was in Dunedin, New Zealand, working in a sleepy university classroom, although what he was investigating wasn't commonly found in universities. His board was packed with mathematical equations that were so foreign it was likely they were alien in design. Part of him wished that thought was just hyperbole. But no, alien was the right word.

Randall rubbed his hands along his forehead and groaned.

How had his life taken such a bizarre turn?

For the hundredth time in the last few days, he went back over the chaotic recent events of his life.

He'd been working in Geneva, Switzerland for a prestigious private research company called Offenes Universum. He was on a scholarship provided by the Australian National University that was incredibly difficult to get. Usually, it was reserved for people finishing their doctorates in maths and physics, but Randall was only one year out of high school. Admittedly, Randall hadn't spent much time actually in high school. He was always at the local university completing extra-credit tasks and assisting professors with complex problems.

All his life he'd been called a prodigy, whatever that meant. Randall just liked numbers. They made sense. He likened long strings of symbols to a column of ants moving along the forest floor. To people, the ants often looked disorganised, wandering aimlessly. Yet, each ant knew its role and what it was achieving. They all contributed to a greater whole; the survival of the colony. Every ant had its place, just like each number in an equation.

When a person can look at it the right way it all fits together.

Randall grinned. Working for Offenes Universum was great. He'd seen some top-secret stuff that he was sure was illegal.

His parents were super proud. His mother, Heidi, was a cleaner and his father, Gary, was an airport truck driver. They never expected to have an award-winning maths geek like Randall for a son. His brothers, on the other hand, only ever seemed to make fun of him.

The only reason Randall was in New Zealand was because of his two older brothers; Josh and Kane.

All three boys had been raised in North Queensland, Australia, in a vibrant tourist town called Cairns. The city had treated them well enough. None of them had ever faced any true adversity and all generally excelled. Moving to Switzerland had caused a lot of doubt and sleepless nights for Randall, but he'd overcome his apprehension. His brothers had been good motivators, in so much as teaching Randall lessons on what not to do. While Randall never tried to talk ill of his brothers, both Josh and Kane were aimless. They certainly hadn't been on bright or fulfilling career trajectories. This spurred Randall into taking a risk and moving overseas.

Kane had recently travelled to Geneva to visit Randall, being unemployed and a little lost with life, as he always was. Randall had managed to get him a guest access pass to Offenes Universum for one day just to check the place out. In all honesty, Randall hadn't known what to do with Kane. In the way that fate waits for the exact right moment to strike, it was during Kane's visit that the current oddness began.

Randall had been showing Kane some of his work when a beautiful woman had burst into his lecture theatre claiming to be a representative of the Australian Government. This woman had been very recognisable. In what was revealed not to be a startling coincidence, she was the ex-girlfriend of Randall's oldest brother, Josh.

With her arrival, Randall's assumption that Josh lived a boring, ordinary life was shattered. The appearance of this woman opened a proverbial book of revelations.

As it turned out, Josh was a werewolf. Like, an actual man who turned into a wolf monster on the full moon. It was a discovery so absurd that Randall still hadn't properly processed it. Werewolves were magic, and he lived in a world of strict science. Not to mention that they were supposed to be entirely fictional.

Yet, minutes after his brother's ex-girlfriend's unexpected appearance, Randall had been attacked by undying demonic cultists. All of a sudden, he was running for his life! Apparently, it was all because of Josh and his monstrous curse. His brother was deeply involved in some grand story of gods and magic, and by sheer blood association, had dragged Randall into his mess.

Naturally, Kane had been there for the supernatural cultist attack. Fortunately for them, the Australians had quite the fighter on their side. The crew the Australian Government had sent to Geneva included a legendary Viking warrior named Sigurd, just to make it all a little more preposterous. Quite the battle had taken place in Randall's office.

Following the lead of the government agents, both Randall and Kane had fought, fled and found themselves on a flight out of the country to Amsterdam.

It was then revealed that the Australian operatives had wanted Randall because of his skills in mathematics. They'd obtained a book full of horrific drawings, occult passages, spells and what looked like complex alien formulas for equations. One of these equations needed to be solved and the agents thought Randall was the man to do it.

With the help of a professor named Malcolm Selleck, Randall had worked all night to translate a certain passage from the book into viable map coordinates. The passage seemed to indicate a place of importance deep in the Pacific Ocean, and Randall had found it.

Now, it seemed, he and Kane were along for the ride. Though, much to his relief, the Dare brothers hadn't been wanted for the submarine journey to those aforementioned coordinates. The Australian team he'd been recruited to assist were somewhere in the depths of the ocean right now, on the verge of discovering something incredible. He and Kane had been left in Dunedin with the Viking warrior Sigurd, and Randall was given the mysterious alien book to study.

Randall yawned loudly, stretching out and turning his attention back to the blackboard.

Despite the cool night-time air in Dunedin, the stuffy university classroom he found himself in was unexpectedly warm. While Randall would have preferred to think the university had an excellent heating system, part of him knew that the abnormal warmth was springing from an unexpected source.

Sitting atop a stack of nearby papers was a heavy black book, the very same book he'd found the coordinates in. According to the Australians, the book's name was Necronomicon, and it was only spoken about in hushed whispers in academic circles. Randall had never heard of it. His work rarely involved old cryptic stories and myths, yet the bizarre string of events that had led to him having the book meant he couldn't pass up this opportunity to study it further.

He had to avert his gaze from the grotesque drawings inside. The passages akin to spells from medieval witchcraft didn't interest Randall remotely. What he found fascinating were the strings of strange symbols that dominated some of the pages. They were most certainly equations written in a long-forgotten language.

Thanks to Malcolm Selleck, the hidden meanings of many of the symbols had been uncovered. He now had a baseline of known characters to work with. Chuffed with his success, Randall had flicked through the book looking for another puzzle to solve. Professor Selleck was currently on the submarine hurtling towards the location they'd uncovered, so Randall was on his own for this one. He liked it better this way. Certainly, the professor had been instrumental in deciphering the ancient symbols, but now that the majority had been determined, Randall could go it on his own.

He still wasn't entirely across what the government was doing. He figured he didn't need to know. Josh seemed to be a government operative himself now, despite being a supernatural monster. Randall had already concluded that Josh was a prisoner of the Australian Government, being used for a mission. The way people avoided eye contact when they called him an 'agent' was very telling. Still, Randall was happy to help where he could.

Tap, tap, tap.

Randall turned to see the dim outline of a gnarled tree branch swaying in the breeze. Every now and then it would softly hit the glass. The repetitive tap, tap, tapping was making Randall feel paranoid. He'd already opened the window and tried to push the branch away, with no success. The tree looked like it was a thousand years old. It was devoid of leaves and twisted at odd angles. The bark was so lumpy in places it appeared as if the old spooky tree was covered in hundreds of staring eyes. The book Randall was currently studying was creepy enough as is, without some ancient tree perpetually stealing his attention away and freaking him out. He couldn't escape the feeling that the tree's knocks were a kind of warning. Like some ancient thing that lived within the old roots wanted him to stop what he was doing...

Randall refocused on his work. He leant so close into the book that his nose almost touched the paper.

The book was strange. Every time Randall touched it, he felt an unfamiliar sense of dread wash over him. Goosebumps raced across his skin and his pulse quickened. He put this down to tricks of his imagination.

Randall ran his hand through his hair.

He was sweating.

He turned away from the blackboard and looked back at the dark window. In the dull lights of the classroom, Randall was perfectly reflected. His hair stuck out at odd angles, and while he could blame the heat in the room, he always looked like that.

Randall was broad-shouldered but extremely skinny. He was tall, lean and gangly, with a thin beard that was turning orange in small patches. His unkempt brown fringe flopped over his forehead as his hazel eyes stared back at him; their depths betraying his inner excitement. His new equation was almost solved.

There was a loud thumping that carried from somewhere down the hall adjacent to his open classroom door. It was probably his brother, Kane, with their new acquaintance, Sigurd. Their training session must've finished.

Randall quickly turned back to the blackboard. He was almost out of time. Kane and Sigurd wouldn't want to wait around for him to finish working.

He looked at his notes and began scribbling hurried numbers on the board.

"Almost there," he muttered.

The voices of Kane and Sigurd were growing louder and louder.

Randall paused, doing a quick series of calculations in his head. The answer was on the tip of his tongue.

"AH HUH!" he exclaimed, almost leaping into the air.

With a slash of his hand, he scrapped his answer out with chalk. The blackboard was full of scribbles incomprehensible to anyone but him. All the math was there, and it was solved, but Randall didn't know what it meant.

His brow again furrowed, Randall stared at the board for several long seconds. He barely noticed the breeze that had whipped up in the room, shooting his untamed strands of hair forward. The pages of the Necronomicon fluttered over one another until a violent gust slammed the book shut.

"What the hell," Randall shouted over the wind, now a roaring gale.

The equation on the blackboard was moving.

Randall rubbed his eyes.

It wasn't a trick of the light. The symbols and numbers were rotating in a circle.

There was a sudden ripping sound, and a glowing tear appeared in the middle of the board. The light inside the tear dissipated quickly, but it grew larger, forming a sphere. The deep black void was spinning clockwise, sucking the wind into it.

Randall squeaked in surprise. Had he somehow opened a black hole in the classroom? If that was the case, then he hadn't only killed himself as a black hole this size would eventually destroy the planet.

"It can't be..." Randall murmured as he gazed into the spinning abyss.

Randall knew that a black hole small enough to fit in the classroom would produce tidal forces so strong that anything nearby would be instantly 'spaghettified', so that couldn't be it. Could this be a wormhole, a bridge across space and time, instead?

The void grew larger and larger. Randall attempted to bolt out of the room but the moment he turned around, to see the shocked looks of Kane and Sigurd in the doorway, he was swept off his feet. Tumbling in mid-air, Randall rolled head-first into the deep black void.

The lights of the classroom vanished as the portal sealed

behind him.

Trapped in infinite black emptiness, Randall held his breath as he zoomed away from Dunedin to destinations unknown.

CHAPTER 2

THE DARK WORLD

Before Randall passed through what he perceived to be the black hole's event horizon; he took in a deep sucking breath of air. Several thoughts crossed his mind at once. The first was that he wasn't stretching. As he suspected, if this was a true black hole, his body should be stretching in its extreme gravity. It had to be a wormhole instead, meaning he may be on his way to somewhere inhospitable to humans. The second was his escape plan. Could he hold his breath long enough to write the equation out again? Could he even remember the equation? He couldn't shake the burning question of how exactly the act of writing out an equation could open a portal? That didn't make any sense at all.

He was embraced by a shroud of the densest blackness he'd ever experienced. He felt a squishing sensation like his body was pushing through a wall of invisible jelly.

Then, there was a hard *thud*.

The journey was over before Randall had properly comprehended it.

Randall landed on his backside. He felt dirt between his fingers. The ground was soft, soft enough to write in!

He could also see. The light was dim, like he was caught in fading twilight.

His mind whirred into action. Without hesitation, Randall dug his pointer finger into the dirt and began drawing.

His face turned red.

He continued scribbling.

His lungs were burning and his vision was growing faint, but he didn't dare stop.

Randall paused. He couldn't remember the next symbol in the sequence!

Desperately holding onto the vanishing air in his lungs, Randall searched his mind for the next portion of the equation.

Nothing!

His body yearned for him to open his mouth and take a breath. Every cell begged him to inhale.

This was it. He was dead.

Resigned to his untimely doom, Randall opened his mouth and let the unknown atmosphere flood into his body. He convulsed, pre-empting the expected choking gasp. But he didn't choke. The air was cool, crisp and oxygenated.

Randall laughed in utter surprise. He could breathe.

The young scientist scrambled to his feet and took several long slow breaths to steady himself. Standing in the dull light he assessed his situation. He knew he wasn't still on Earth. His body felt lighter. With a hopping bounce, he jumped, shooting higher into the air than he normally would. This place had a different gravity. He was on an alien world!

Almost instinctively Randall looked at the stars. For generations untold, the sky had provided humans with guidance from the infinite heavens. The primeval comfort of the milky way wasn't in this place. Terror welled in Randall's chest as he stared up at the black void. There weren't stars up there, instead strange lights periodically pulsed up high. They were like squashed dim ovals that infrequently lit up, igniting the blackness. It was unlike anything Randall had ever seen or read about. Even with his understanding of astrophysics (limited though it was), he had no explanations for the strange lights hovering above this dark world.

He sucked in another fearful breath and tried to quell the rising panic inside.

"What can I do?" Randall thought. There wasn't a problem he couldn't solve. All that was needed was the appropriate application of proper logic.

This planet was oxygen-rich, meaning it was like Earth. There could be life here... intelligent life even. Because the Necronomicon had brought him here, it was highly likely that there were aliens smart enough to read and write. This place could be the origin of the mysterious book. Perhaps there were other lost travellers like him? There was no reason to assume there wasn't, though by the same token, there was no reason to assume there was.

Randall scratched his chin nervously. He needed to get his bearings; a task easier said than done on another planet.

He turned his gaze from the sky and towards his surroundings. At first glance, it looked like he was standing in a sparse forest. Though the closer he looked, the more he could see how odd the trees were. Unlike the trees of Earth, which were protected with bark, these manifestations of flora were fleshy in texture and purple in colour. They had branches but no leaves, and each bend in them was jarringly smooth.

"Okay... I am in an inflatable forest," Randall muttered quietly.

His quiet comment was met with a distant high-pitched screech.

Randall clasped his hands to his mouth.

The screech set off a chorus of wailing cries in all directions. The pained shouts filled the still air. Some sounded a little too close.

Randall's knees started shuddering so violently they gave out and he collapsed into the dirt. He could feel a panic attack coming.

"Now... is... not... the... time!" Randall told himself. He swallowed his fear and took some calming breaths. Within a minute, Randall was composed, though he was still lying in the dirt, curled in a ball.

There was a sound like footsteps shuffling nearby.

Randall jumped to his feet and scanned left to right. He couldn't see far in any direction. The pulsing lights above weren't bright enough.

Nothing moved, yet Randall couldn't escape the feeling that

he was being watched.

At least whatever had moved in the dark nearby wasn't screeching or wailing. It was a small comfort in this dreadful place.

Randall spent several long minutes in that spot, scanning the darkness around him for shapes. Realising that if he was being watched, the watcher wasn't going to willingly reveal themselves; Randall decided to move.

To his right, the ground tilted downwards and the trees grew denser. It was far blacker that way. To his left, the ground seemed to rise. If he went left, perhaps he could find a hill or a lookout. It felt like the more appropriate choice. If there were civilisations out here, they would surely have fire at the bare minimum, or so Randall hoped. A distant orange glow could be his salvation if he could spot it.

He wondered how well he'd be able to communicate with alien beings huddled around a fire. Physics wasn't just equations. It revealed the very laws of the universe. And he knew how some of the symbols had been represented by the Necronomicon. That was the key to speaking out here, the symbols from the book. But even then, he'd have to gamble on encountering creatures advanced enough to recognise what he was trying to say. It was all very worrisome.

Feeling unsure of himself, Randall began walking. Those first few steps took great courage. With each stride, Randall felt like he was winning a small victory against his fear.

The lighter gravity made Randall's trudge uphill easy at least. He was almost skipping in time to the pulses of the lights above.

Randall's mind drifted to the wormhole he'd miraculously created in Dunedin. The idea of a portal connecting two different points in spacetime wasn't crazy. Such concepts were introduced by Einstein and Rosen over a hundred years ago. The basic principle was that the fabric of spacetime became so severely warped that ordinarily disparate locations connected. Of course, it was all theoretical.

"Well… was theoretical," Randall grinned.

How it worked and why it had happened felt like mysteries that were beyond Randall's understanding right now.

The chorus of wails, both near and far, sprang up at random intervals in the fleshy forest. Bat-winged creatures fluttered about above the trees, giving Randall little frights every time he heard the flapping of their leathery appendages. He couldn't get a good look at them but wasn't disappointed with that. He hoped that whatever life had evolved here was small and unthreatening. For all he knew, the flying monsters high above were hungry pterodactyls. Instead of dwelling on that dreadful potential, images of fluffy pink cat-like creatures danced through Randall's mind. He chuckled at the thought of his imagined cat aliens worshipping him as a foreign god.

"What are the chances of that? Considering I am currently on an alien planet, the odds can't be that bad…" Randall thought.

Randall had no way to tell the passing of time and soon became acutely aware of the fact that he had no idea how long he'd been walking. His legs ached and his eyes drooped. At some point, a pleasant surprise had manifested itself in the form of Earthly trees slowly appearing among the fleshy alien ones. They weren't entirely familiar, as they still looked far too smooth, but at least they had dense foliage. It was a small comfort and Randall embraced it.

His nerves didn't abate with the walk, though. It was like he was carrying a solid weight in his stomach the entire journey uphill. Deep breathing techniques he'd learned from childhood psychologists, designed to help with anxiety, provided no relief.

Here he was on an alien planet! Randall certainly couldn't deny the small thrill buried beneath mountains of fear. It was that spark of excitement that kept him moving, but damn was he tired.

A particularly bright flash ignited the forest from above. It revealed a clearing just ahead. Mustering his depleted energy reserves, Randall rushed forward. He slid between two slimy trees and emerged at the edge of a precipice.

Randall gasped.

He was high atop a sheer cliff face looking at an enormous crater below. It was as if a giant hand had reached down and scooped a chunk of the countryside away. The hole stretched far into the distance, well beyond the visible horizon, and was so black its internal mysteries could never be spied from the outside.

Randall looked at the curious pulsing lights igniting the landscape. He hadn't had a good view from the forest. There were hundreds of dim ovals high up in the sky, flashing at random. Another source of light was also apparent here too. Far below, around the edge of the crater, was a cluster of ruined buildings emitting a dull green glow. They appeared to be a series of ancient gates and ziggurats in varying states of disrepair. Smaller structures of sandstone were caught in their dull gleam.

There was something worrisome about the buildings, though Randall couldn't work out what exactly it was that made him feel so uneasy. The architecture was strange. It seemed to bend and warp as he gazed at it. Some of the ziggurats looked as if they'd once connected to bridge-ways that'd been swallowed by the crater.

He pushed his nervousness aside. The ruins were the first sign of civilisation he'd come across and it was in his best interest to investigate them. He could see from his vantage point that if he continued along the cliff face, he'd go downhill, and then it was a simple sharp right turn to the ruins. He desperately wanted to sleep, refresh his brain and properly assess his situation from a place of safety and shelter.

Tiredness his guide, Randall marched on at a hurried pace. While he wanted to continue on the outer edge of the trees to keep the ruins in sight, that quickly became impossible. The trees became thicker and more tangled the further downhill he travelled. He had to push through heavy vines suffocating the dense undergrowth.

The terrain evened out, and Randall knew that if he turned right the ruins should soon come into view. He just had to be careful not to walk straight into the crater in the low light.

Randall pushed through a slick wall of fleshy vines and came to an abrupt halt.

Not more than twenty yards ahead, shrouded in the dark of the trees were three shapes… humanoid shapes! It looked like there were three people in conversation just ahead of him!

"HELLO!" Randall shouted enthusiastically.

He rushed forward, losing his footing and tripping. Randall spat dirt as he collected himself, looking to see if the other people had heard him.

Right as Randall pushed himself to his knees, the floating ovals above blazed with intensity, flooding the forest with a prolonged burst of light.

Horror overtook Randall. He could see the closest of the silhouettes clearly now.

The creature was eerily pale. Its skin was translucent, revealing a tangled web of blue veins covering depleted muscles. Disgusting thick globs of slime fell periodically down its arms. Randall's eyes flicked to the bones of its humanoid spinal column, which he could see clearly as prominent ridges running along its back. It looked sunken and drowned, like a corpse that'd been too long underwater reanimated.

The three creatures remained frozen, their backs still to Randall. Randall could only assume the other two, both still shrouded in darkness, looked like the visible monster.

"Maybe they didn't hear me," Randall dared to dream.

No, that was impossible. His shout had carried through the night. It was like these things were still processing it.

The closest of them turned on the spot.

It was a monster.

Its head came into clear view. It was like a zombie. There were no gums around its mouth, just raw flesh besides elongated horse teeth. Its eyelids sagged so far along its face that there was no way they could be closed. Most horrifying were the blank orb-like eyes devoid of any detail. The right side of its temple looked like it'd been caved in with a baseball bat. The rest of its body was misshapen too. Its torso consisted of loose skin over bone. Randall noticed its shoulders were not symmetrical, with the left sitting far higher than the right.

The creature screamed.

It was the same ghastly wailing he'd heard all through his journey in the forest.

Randall froze. His heart beat in his ears. He willed himself to move but he couldn't.

"Move, dammit!" Randall commanded his legs. But nothing happened. He was rooted to the spot.

The abomination limped towards him with surprising speed. The other two things followed close behind.

The lights from above faded and the forest returned to its usual gloom. Out of the corner of his eye, Randall noticed a green glow. The ruins were nearby.

The ragged breathing of the creatures filled the air. Their stink flowed into Randall's nostrils. The vacant-eyed zombie reached out for him with its misshapen fingers.

"Move, you fool!" a voice called inside Randall's head.

Randall clumsily rolled to the side, the creature's slimy hand scraping the side of his face. It felt like a putrid wet slap across the cheek.

"RUN!" the inner voice howled.

Randall bolted.

He needed every ounce of concentration he possessed not to stumble as he swerved around trees and through vines. He could hear the monsters matching his every movement, keeping pace with him. Randall was always lanky and uncoordinated, though he'd never imagined his slow reaction times would get him killed by zombies.

Randall passed through the shadow of a large sandstone arch. Before him were several structures evenly spaced across a flat expanse of earth. The collection of green buildings emitted a haunting ghostly light, filling the area with a sinister fog. Directly ahead was what looked like a partially-standing temple complex consisting of interwoven buildings linked with dark alleys.

"I can get lost in there!" Randall thought, forcing himself into a harrowing sprint.

Randall didn't dare look back. He suspected that on open terrain he was faster than the creatures, as he couldn't hear their strangled gurgling behind him anymore. Randall passed by a looming ziggurat and felt uneasy. The building carried with it a loathsome dread. Unspeakable terrors from ancient aeons lingered like emotional stains on the brickwork. It rose high above Randall, twisted and alien, warning him not to be here. Randall turned right around the ziggurat and then careened into the shadows of the nearest alley dividing the temple complex.

The alley turned left and ascended a small flight of stairs before ending at a stone door. Randall gripped the large bronze handle and pulled with all his might. Much to his surprise, the door slid open without a sound. He paused before stepping inside, unable to quell the sense of fear this place generated. Going inside didn't feel like the right thing to do. But, by the same token, staying out with the zombies wasn't a good option either. Randall's view of the way he'd come from was blocked by a large stone wall topped with a series of thick columns. He could reach the top and climb up, if he wanted to. Perhaps it'd allow him to see if the zombies were still following him.

Randall carefully pulled himself atop the wall, positioning himself behind a column. He had a perfect view of the clearing he'd just sprinted through. Ambling across that same space were the three disfigured zombies, turning back and forth, scanning all around with their vacant orb-like eyes.

The lead zombie let out a horrifying wail that bounced off the surrounding buildings and sunk into the green fog. This spooked Randall enough to make up his mind. He was heading inside, at least only for as long as these things were going to hang around.

Resolute, Randall intended on moving, but a new sound answered the zombies' wail.

Click, click, click.

Something else was in the clearing.

There was a thud and a snap as a large body smashed into the lead zombie. The zombie shrieked horrifically as its skin was stripped from its bones. The other two zombies lumbered forward aggressively, but the new creature reacted quickly, pouncing on the first, then turning towards the other.

It was hard for Randall to see what the attacker was. The green fog appeared to cling to and thicken around this foe.

The new monster looked roughly humanoid, though a series of thin waving limbs attached to its head indicated that it wasn't a person.

Despite being grievously injured, the first zombie staggered to its feet in a desperate attempt to continue its attack.

The fighting drew closer to Randall.

He could see all the combatants clearly now.

The new monster had the rough body shape of a slender gorilla. It was hunched and coated in thick muscle beneath slimy greyish-green skin. It had a cephalopod head with small black eyes and long tentacles where a mouth should be. The most powerful of its tentacles were the four lined with hooks and suckers springing from its back. Randall noticed that one of the upper back tentacles was damaged, appearing like it'd been chopped in half. The monster was somewhat aquatic in appearance, but also draconic. It was an octopus-man.

The attacker gripped one of the zombies with both of its clawed hands and ripped it clean in half. Steaming entrails collapsed in a heap on the ground as the zombie continued its loud wailing, as if its sudden reduction in size meant nothing.

Using one of its powerful back tentacles, the octo-man ripped the downed zombie's head off and held it high. It was warning the other zombies away. It turned in a full circle, and for a horrifying second, paused when it looked in Randall's direction.

He'd lingered too long. Randall had to go now.

He slid back down the wall and ducked behind the stone door, pulling it closed behind him and embracing the horror of the ruins.

CHAPTER 3

THE RUINS OF R'LYEH

Randall took a deep breath in a futile attempt to steady himself. His heart pounded so loudly in his ears that he was deaf to all other sounds.

What had that creature been? And more importantly, had it seen him?

He sank to his knees and fought back tears. He wasn't meant to be here, in this horrible place. What dreadful luck had brought him into this dark world? Though it wasn't entirely dark inside the ruin. In fact, he could see better here than outside.

Randall took stock of his surroundings.

He was in a long rectangular hallway that gently sloped downwards before coming to an abrupt turn about two hundred metres ahead. While there was no obvious light source, the place shone with a dim glow that shimmered out of the walls.

The internal structure was made of the same loathsome deep

green stone that warped his senses and twisted his mind. On his right and left were carvings depicting the stories of alien things. It was reminiscent of the art of ancient Egypt, though far more intricate and devoid of colour.

Randall shuddered as he traced his finger along the image of a human-like creature with bulbous eyes and a fish head.

From the hilltop, the ruins had seemed abandoned, yet that monstrous octopus-headed being had proven his assumption wrong. Perhaps his other guesses were wrong, too? While it appeared as if the collection of buildings before the enormous crater were the leftovers of some cataclysm that had destroyed the city proper; he had to now consider that the rest of the place could be in the depths of that crater. This downward-sloping tunnel may take him there. Into the abyss...

He didn't really want to venture into the crater.

There were no good options. He could follow the tunnel into a potential labyrinth and become food for whatever creatures dwelled in the ghostly green halls. Or, he could attempt to leave his ruinous haven and take his chances back in the forest.

"What do I know?" Randall murmured to himself.

That was easy. He knew there were monsters outside. So far, he had no data to suggest there were monsters inside. It was never a good idea to formulate plans from incomplete data, but he didn't see much of a choice. He'd travel down the tunnel and assess what he found. At least he could see well enough, and other than his heaving breaths, there was dead silence.

The hall was easily high enough for him to walk comfortably. Randall was worried that each footfall would echo horribly off the stone walls like the repeated banging of an obnoxious gong, announcing his presence to any dwellers in the dark. That didn't come to be, much to his relief. The shimmering green floor absorbed the sound.

Randall proceeded slowly. Several times he thought he heard running water beneath him, and once a far-off banging. He slowed his pace even more, but didn't stop. When he came to branches in the path he chose to go right. If he always went right then he could always find his way back.

He'd expected to come across statues and religious relics, though, other than the art on the walls, the place was devoid of detail. Randall was also unnerved by the fact that there was no dust or cobwebs. There was only the long green path downwards.

When at last the hallway split into a series of adjacent rooms, Randall decided to investigate the first one. He carefully nudged a heavy stone door open and was surprised to find collections of clunky machinery inside, still turning and whirring. It was like nothing he'd ever seen on Earth, so couldn't begin to guess if it was primitive or advanced. Large bronze pipes dominated the rear wall, plunging through the floor into unknown depths. He even found what looked to be control panels, though they were lifeless. Steeling his nerve, he touched the side of a silver metal box containing a series of dead lights. It was cool to the touch and surprisingly soft. The metal moved with his finger as if it was water.

"Nanotech, or potentially biological," Randall thought.

While the room was predominantly green, there were jarring portions of yellow too. Flat examination tables and panels in the wall stood out in stark contrast to the original design. Randall wondered just how old this place was? Clearly, the ruins had been around long enough to require addition and modification at some point. Yet they couldn't be ancient, as some of the machinery still worked.

One of the yellow stone panels caught Randall's eye. It featured a spiral pattern of small holes on its face and looked different from the rest of the wall. Randall moved towards it and knelt down. He could feel air being sucked through it. It was also slightly ajar from the wall; if he wanted to, he could dig his fingers in and remove it. This was potentially a maintenance hatch or air vent.

Randall frowned. He'd assumed the creature guarding the ruins was an animal, due to its lack of clothes or weapons. But, perhaps not. If it was a descendant of whatever had built all this, it was most certainly intelligent.

Somehow, that wasn't comforting.

Click, click, click.

Randall froze.

Click, click, click.

It was coming closer. The clicking was coming from down the hallway. It was the same sound the octopus-man outside had made. One of those creatures was here!

Randall looked at the ajar stone door. It'd immediately know that someone had entered this room. He had to hide, but where?

Fear rose like a king tide inside him. The hulking humanoid octopus alien would rip him apart like he was made of paper. Randall scanned the room from left to right. His eyes came to rest on the stone with the spiral pattern. It was the vent he'd discovered moments ago!

Randall tip-toed over to the yellow slab, desperate not to make any noise. Pushing his fingers into the groove between the stone and the wall, Randall pulled it forward. It was heavy and scraped along the ground.

A series of furious clicks echoed out from nearby. They were louder now... closer...

Randall crouched and slid into the now open hole in the wall. It was completely dark inside.

His hands shaking, Randall fumbled to pull the slab closed behind him. Cool air brushed against the sweat on his skin.

The holes in the stone were too small to see through, so maintaining his crouch, Randall backed away slowly.

The door to the larger room was loudly and violently thrust open as a chorus of clicks filled the room. Randall turned around as quietly as he could and moved into the darkness of the vent.

It was slow going as Randall felt his way forward blindly. The air had a metallic taste to it that left Randall's teeth feeling fuzzy. Who knew what alien gasses were being pumped through here. He longed for a sliver of light to appear so he could see where he was going.

Randall yelped as his right foot plunged into nothingness. Taken entirely by surprise, Randall tumbled forward into empty space.

The fall was short and Randall was amazed to be able to stagger upright uninjured. There was enough room for Randall to stand, and if he jumped his fingers could touch the upper vent he'd fallen through. However, his hands feeling the wall ahead told him he'd have to continue crouching to follow this new path. He didn't even have to debate with himself about turning back. Randall again began crouching through the blackness. When he navigated a sharp left turn, he was amazed to finally see small pockets of light shining through holes in the ground.

Randall scrambled forward, the light feeling like an old friend he'd lost long ago. It was hope manifested in the dark.

Again, holes were cut in a spiral pattern, though these holes were large enough to see through. Randall could get a good glimpse of what was below.

He saw the familiar glowing green of the architecture along with scattered artefacts on the floor. They looked like workman's tools.

Randall crawled down the vent a few more feet and looked through the next spiral.

There was a kind of thick glass tube bolted to the ground. Each end looked similar in shape to an aircraft engine, with hatches open to reveal complex electronics inside. It appeared as if someone, or something, was performing maintenance on it. Randall's first thought was that the tube was a medical device, designed to house a living being inside.

Randall moved again.

He gasped. Now he saw a white platform beside a steep pit that dove deep into the ground. It looked like an elevator of sorts. He could also see the outer edges of more medical devices layered on top of one another.

Randall proceeded to the last spiral and peered down.

Directly below him were rows of man-sized glass tubes, except these were active. Beneath the cloudy glass exteriors of the tubes were humanoid shadows encased in bubbling liquid. Randall peered intently down, trying to properly discern what he was seeing. An intuitive part of him already knew what was inside each tube.

They were the same as the octopus creature from earlier. There must've been hundreds of them in neatly-stacked rows descending into the depths.

"These are cryo chambers," Randall deduced. They were chambers designed to hold the organisms inside in an indefinite stasis. There was a preserved army resting in these ruins. How old were they? Clearly, some of their soldiers were awake, both guarding the ruins and performing maintenance work.

Randall thought he saw one of the figures in the tubes stir, which caused his heart to leap out of his chest. The terrifying thought of being trapped with a newly awoken horde of octo-men played on repeat in his head. Desiring to be free of this waking nightmare, he hurried on. Randall would've preferred to think that the creatures in the tubes were preserved specimens of a bygone race, making this a kind of catacomb. Seeing them stir in their sleep was not pleasant.

Back in the pitch black and left to his own wild speculations, Randall continued his slow descent as the tunnel tilted downward, diving further into the crater.

Randall figured at least an hour passed before something new broke the monotony of the journey.

A low electronic hum rumbled through the stale air. It was

accompanied by a wet slapping sound, almost like large slimy creatures were belly-flopping onto the floor of a nearby echoing chamber.

"This must be the end of the tunnel," Randall assured himself quietly.

The persistent crouch he'd maintained to get through the small space was beginning to wreak havoc on his knees. Reluctantly, Randall decided that he'd have to get on his stomach and army crawl forward. His upper body strength certainly left something to be desired as he pulled himself across the ancient stone.

The sounds grew louder as the tunnel became brighter. Light was flooding in.

This place was no sleepy catacomb. Things were moving somewhere ahead.

Click, click, click.

There it was again. The methodical insect-like clicking of the octopus creatures. He imagined that hidden somewhere beneath their swathes of tentacles was a beak. The dreadful sound caused Randall to briefly pause. Did he want to see what was at the end of this tunnel?

Though, the clicks weren't close. It sounded like they were travelling up the stone walls from somewhere below. Plus, he couldn't have crawled and crouched this far without satiating his curiosity. Octopus monsters behind him and octopus monsters ahead. He might as well go forward.

Randall followed a bend in the tunnel and came face to face with a problem. A yellow slab of stone blocked the path forward. It looked cut with a series of layered rectangles lined with grooves allowing the air to pass through.

The air here was thick and carried with it a foul smell.

"This is definitely a vent," Randall grinned. He was pleased to have his earlier guess confirmed. He wiped the smile from his face when he imagined how foolish he must look. Randall's situation couldn't be more dire.

He pulled himself as close as he could to one of the larger grooves in the stone and peered through it. What confronted him was equal parts terrifying and spectacular.

He was looking out on an expansive room dominated by a central raised platform. Randall ogled the structure. This was no ancient ruin nor decorative art piece. It was a multi-level computer of sorts, lit with blinking, coloured lights and emitting a low shrill hum. It was made of two circular pieces, though the bottom circle was far wider than the top one.

Atop the higher level were two gleaming black columns, tapered at the top and curved inwards to look like menacing pincers. They sparked with electrical energy.

Thick oily cabling spread from the bottom circular platform to large mainframe towers nestled in purpose-designed compartments in the far wall. The device had abundant wires flowing from it in all directions; wires that squirmed and writhed as if they were alive. But the wires had nothing on the eyes... As the platforms slowly rotated anti-clockwise, Randall was perplexed to see large splodges of organic matter stuck to the device like mud on a boot. Each of these unholy attachments were full of eyes of different types and sizes. They blinked at random and scanned the room. Some even had small waving tentacles bursting from their free space. Other pockets of biological matter oozed and bubbled on the machinery. Randall's first thought was these odd things were parasites attracted to whatever energy powered this machine.

And the smell! The smell was rotten beyond comprehension. Randall couldn't describe it even if he wanted to.

Randall breathed through his mouth to escape the stench. He deduced the source of the monstrous odour quickly.

The walls were lined with hundreds of the same pods he'd seen earlier. Each monstrous occupant was visible behind a cloudy glass casing.

An army rested in these ruins.

The origin of the wet-slapping sounds he'd heard became obvious too. The floor was covered in large green tentacles flailing, twisting and contorting. They wriggled and reached over one another, making it look like the ground level was alive with impossibly thick snakes. The tentacles had even found footholds in between the layers of stasis pods. It was an infestation.

Randall shuddered at the thought of sinking beneath the mass below. Did the tentacles guard the central device? And what did it do?

Click, click, click.

One of the creatures was here.

The floor-level tentacles parted as the octo-man strode towards the central device. It had appeared from somewhere directly below Randall, meaning the entry to this room must be accessible from the same direction he'd come. That could be important.

This creature wasn't lurking or prowling. It walked upright, though heavily hunched, approaching the machine with confidence.

Even from his high vantage point, Randall could plainly see the creature's body change as it drew closer to the sparkling black pincers. Its soft green flesh mutated; hardening. This was clearly a defensive adaptation. Thick ridges formed on its head and armour plates emerged across its shoulders and back. Small spikes, that glowed a bright green, lined each bony plate.

Perhaps this room was dangerous for the octo-men?

The creature stopped short of the lower platform and let out a retching cry. Randall pressed his hands against his ears and braced against the sound. The floor-level tentacles didn't like this sound, as they all slithered down into the holes from which they sprang. The organic matter containing eyes responded differently. The clumps of them on the machine seemed to dissolve and swirl through the air.

Randall backed away quickly. They weren't going to come through his air vent, were they?

After a minute had passed with Randall compressing himself against the wall, he dared to look back down.

The matter had clumped at the foot of the octo-man, becoming a fleshy stand that supported a flat square of eyes. The eyes swivelled as the octo-man placed his armoured hand in the centre of the pad.

The entire chamber was engulfed by a green hologram. Spinning before Randall in mid-air, like a ghostly apparition, was the planet Earth.

The control apparatus had taken on the appearance of a screen, like a tablet computer on a stand made of tendons.

The octopus creature again pressed its gnarled hand to the screen and the hologram moved. It zoomed in on Australia. An area, in the general vicinity of where Randall thought Sydney should be, lit up like a beacon.

Then, the machine whirred to life. Electricity crackled between the two pincers, growing in brightness and intensity. The arching lines flew across open space and met one another in mid-air. It was like the lightning was forming a mesh gate between the two black columns.

"It's a door!" Randall breathed, subduing his inner excitement. Not just a door, but a portal! Perhaps a portal across space or dimensions! He was willing to bet his life savings that the same physics from the Necronomicon that brought him here powered this gateway.

The previous low hum grew into a loud chorus and the platforms spun quickly. Lightning bathed the octo-man, doing little damage as it struck the creature's biological armour.

There was an explosion of sparks and the central platforms stopped spinning. The electronic humming died away and was replaced with the furious clicking of the octopus below. The device hadn't worked.

Randall frowned. This presented quite a conundrum. Through sheer luck alone he'd found a way back to his world, or so he guessed, but the way back wasn't yet ready. He couldn't stay in this tunnel and wait, could he? No. He needed to eat, drink and sleep. Plus, even if he could remove the stone slab in front of him, it was a drop of at least 40 metres to the ground. Even then, he'd have to navigate a maze of tentacles before he could pass through the gateway. There had to be a better way.

For the briefest moment, hopelessness washed over Randall Dare. He was truly alone here.

"No, stop. Enough," Randall told himself. Even if he was a victim of circumstance, accepting the designation of 'victim' never got anyone anywhere. He was going to find a way out of this.

There was a sound like an engine revving. Randall again peered down to see a metal plate embedded in the ground spinning quickly. The octo-man had been standing on it, but now quickly moved aside as a beam of light shot straight up from that spot. Inside the pillar of light was a swirling cloud of particles. The tumbling cloud grew in size over several seconds until another flash ignited the room and a second octo-man emerged.

The two creatures clicked at each other as their facial tentacles touched in greeting. The original creature beckoned the other one over to the central device to inspect it.

"A second scientist, perhaps," Randall considered. His eyes flicked to the metallic plate. It was still spinning away, generating the pillar of light. The teleport was still active... but where did it go?

Randall gazed down at the newly emerged octo-man. There was something recognisable about this one. The upper right tentacle on its back had been cut in half! This was the monster that had attacked the zombies outside! Therefore, the teleport had to lead somewhere close to where he'd entered the ruins from.

Randall only now noticed that the creeping tentacles that had vanished when the central device activated were now creeping back up the walls and filling the empty spaces on the floor. A daring plan occurred to him. But did he have the courage to do it? He was so tired that fear and logic no longer concerned him. He just needed to get away.

"I'm not dying in this vent, I know that much," Randall grimaced.

While he was comfortable in the realm of thinking, now was the time for action. With a little bit of luck, he could get out of here.

Generating as much power as he could, Randall kicked with both feet, sending the yellow stone slab flying outwards.

Randall spun his body around and flung himself out of the small hole legs first. Holding on for dear life by the tips of his fingers, Randall scanned the walls on either side of him.

Yes! One long thick tentacle was snaking its way up the wall just to his right. Randall reached out and wrapped his right arm around it, causing the tentacle to violently shudder and twitch. He released his hold of the vent and slid down the tentacle to ground level, collapsing onto his rear end.

The octo-men moved to attack. Right as they pounced, Randall dived in the direction of the pillar of light, though it was too far away. He avoided the attack, performing an unintended gangly summersault, before getting to his feet. One of the floor tentacles wrapped around his foot, and Randall stamped on it furiously. Its suckers released and Randall sprinted like he'd never sprinted before.

With the leap of an accomplished gymnast, he soared into

the light. A woozy sensation washed over him as the room disappeared in a flash.

A few seconds passed, and once again Randall was outside. He found himself in the crumbling ruins of a small shrine defined by four columns that had once held up a now-vanished roof.

Randall stepped from the light and looked at the metal teleportation plate. He needed a way to stop the octo-creatures from following him. Without thinking, he reached for a nearby brick and brought it down on the edge of the plate with all his might. The plate cracked, and then the light faded.

He'd done it! But now wasn't the time to celebrate his miraculous escape. He needed to get the hell away from these ruins.

Randall ran for the tree line.

He left the dimly glowing buildings and the haunting mist behind as he was once again engulfed by the tangled web of fleshy flora.

He paused to catch his breath. Sweat fell like rain from his temple and burned like acid in his eyes.

CRACK!

Something else was here…

Humanoid silhouettes were emerging from the trees all around Randall. More of the zombies, probably attracted by the noise from earlier, had arrived. A chorus of horrific wails filled the air. There was no getting out of this one. Randall Dare's luck had at last run out.

ROOAAARRRRR!

The wailing stopped, entirely overcome by a new sound. A

deep bellowing roar burst through the trees, bringing with it the sound of heavy footsteps and breaking branches.

A dark shape was approaching quickly, knocking the vegetation askew. It was huge.

The lights high above shined bright, and Randall was again caught in total disbelief.

The thing that was coming… was a T-Rex.

Its attack was swift and brutal. Enormous powerful jaws clamped down on the first zombie while its tail swept through the undergrowth, knocking several others away.

Randall marvelled at the dinosaur. It towered above him, an ode to the majesty of Earth's ancient past. Its dark brown scaly skin and yellow reptilian eyes were unfriendly. At once, Randall knew who owned this forest, and that he was not welcome.

The zombies united against this new primeval foe, attempting to claw up its leathery hide. The dinosaur simply squashed them beneath its clawed feet. They couldn't do anything against this ancient terror.

The T-Rex bellowed again and the remaining zombies scarpered off into the night.

The dinosaur turned, locking its reptilian eyes on Randall.

Randall squeaked, frozen with fear as this new threat took a thundering step towards him.

There was no escaping now. This was not a foe Randall could overcome.

CHAPTER 4

THE DINOSAUR KING

Never had a man felt smaller than Randall did as he cowered beneath the looming dinosaur. He closed his eyes and braced for a bite. One swift chomp and it would all be over. He knew the T-Rex had the greatest bite force of any animal to walk the Earth, so at least it would be quick.

"First human on an alien planet and first human to be eaten by a dinosaur," Randall thought glumly. The absurd juxtaposition wasn't lost on him.

The bite didn't come. A minute passed as Randall sat there with his eyes closed, meek and scared in the dirt.

He felt a wave of hot breath wash over him before something leathery pressed against the side of his face. The T-Rex was sniffing him!

"New to the Dark World, aren't you?" the dinosaur asked, with the barest hint of a smirk on its jaws.

Randall was so stunned he couldn't respond.

The dinosaur took a thundering step back.

"You can talk?" Randall breathed.

"As can you," the dinosaur laughed. Its mouth moved as if it were speaking in a human manner, though that couldn't be possible. The vocal cords of the ancient carnivore shouldn't have been able to replicate human speech.

Then, Randall saw it. He hadn't noticed it in all the action, but the right side of the dinosaur's enormous head was coated in a parasitic growth. Bubbling eyes and waving tentacles burst from deep green patches on its leathery skin. This dinosaur was infected, like the portal room in the ruins had been.

Randall scrambled to his feet. "You're not going to eat me, are you?"

"I have no desire to feel your tendons between my teeth," the dinosaur grinned. His voice was deep yet held a surprising jovial spark in it.

"You're a dinosaur," Randall stated, immediately feeling stupid.

"And you are a pink hairless ape of impressive mental ability," the T-Rex responded.

"Does he mean me specifically or humans in general," Randall wondered.

"There are ways to know when foreigners come to this place. I've been searching the forests for some time now, thought the wailers might've gotten to you first," the dinosaur explained.

"What is this place?" Randall asked, more to himself in total exasperation than to the dinosaur. He was frustrated. Alien ruins, octopus-men and now a T-Rex. It was like he had stepped into a simulation instead of a real place. He was in the imagination of a child smashing random toys together.

"I suppose you haven't received an introduction yet. Let's get the big picture things out of the way. This planet is called the Dark World. You are from the physical universe; we are no longer in the physical universe. My name is Tyrannogod, the Dinosaur King."

"Tyrannogod... the Dinosaur King..." Randall repeated slowly. For a creature that should be 65 million years old, that name was far too modern. And, it was silly. The fearsome dinosaur had a silly name.

"That is my name. What is yours?" Tyrannogod waited patiently for a response.

"Oh, um, Randall Dare," he answered.

"Randall Dare from Earth, the pleasure is mine. I'd shake your hand, but considering..." Tyrannogod waved his tiny two-fingered forelimb up and down.

"You know I'm from Earth?" Randall asked, suppressing a sudden urge to laugh.

"You are not the first human to set foot here. I must say, it is always a pleasure when a being from my own world arrives. Though we are separated by long stretches of time, we are still brothers, in a way."

Randall was disappointed. He wasn't the first man to walk on an alien world then. It made sense, though. The Necronomicon had been around for some time and others would've figured out its secrets before.

"I have so many questions," Randall began, but Tyrannogod cut him off.

"Come with me, out of the forest and away from the ruins of R'lyeh. It is not safe here. Those wailers will return in greater numbers if we linger."

Randall could hear snapping twigs nearby as creatures moved in the darkness around them.

Tyrannogod collapsed to the ground. His big reptilian eyes glared intently at Randall.

He didn't know what to do. He just stared at the dinosaur.

"Climb onto my back," Tyrannogod sighed. "I don't like to act as transport for smaller beings, but the going will be too slow. We have a distance to traverse."

Randall nodded. In a world with no good options, he figured he might as well take the opportunity to ride a dinosaur while it was there.

He approached the dinosaur. He imagined it was like hopping on the back of a large horse. Randall clambered up the dinosaur's side and swung his leg over the base of his neck.

Tyrannogod grunted and rose to his feet, Randall swaying violently and gripping on for dear life. He was riding a dinosaur.

"Those white zombie things that attacked me... what are they?" Randall asked over Tyrannogod's thundering steps.

"We call them the wailers, those creatures. Abominations they are," Tyrannogod growled.

"Are they from Earth, like us?"

"No, they are from the Dark World. When beings, like you humans, are first introduced to outer god magic, they will inevitably pull wailers into their dimension. They don't need to eat, drink, or sleep and can last for centuries. All they do is stand there and wail when in captivity. Though, in saying that, as they are broken and terrible creatures, they do often die at random."

Randall didn't understand most of what was just said.

"What is outer god magic?" he asked.

"For a being that has come to the Dark World you know very little of the forces you are playing with," Tyrannogod replied, sounding both shocked and intrigued.

"I know nothing about any of it," Randall said honestly. "I was given a book with an equation in it. I wrote the equation down, solved it, and ended up here. You said earlier that we were outside the physical universe; what does that mean?"

Tyrannogod paused. Randall thought the dinosaur might be best contemplating how to explain the unexplainable.

A bright idea came to Randall. He could make this a little easier for his new companion and pick up some critical pieces of the story along the way.

"Tell me your story, Tyrannogod. How has a dinosaur ended up here, still alive after such a long time?" Randall asked.

"A long time hardly does it justice. I know my kind ended. How long has it been in your era?"

"65 million years," Randall answered promptly.

"Longer than memory itself," Tyrannogod stated sadly. "I was once a beast. I walked the Earth, stalking and hunting my prey. Then, *he* found me. He made me his plaything. An experiment. A mutation."

"Who is he?" Randall asked.

"Nyarlathotep, the outer god," Tyrannogod spat. "No doubt you have seen the gifts of his touch on my skin."

Randall leaned over to look at the bubbling pool of eyes wobbling in all directions.

"I've never heard of an outer god, but I am guessing it's an alien concept. Like a god not from the Earth," Randall said.

"Correct, in a way. You will meet many of us who have felt the fearsome sting of the outer gods. Whether it be Nyarlathotep or Yog-Sothoth, the same story is repeated a thousand times in the Dark World."

Randall had actually met a god. He'd travelled in the company of the Greek Goddess Artemis, though hadn't really spoken to her. From what he'd picked up, she was only a few thousand years old, which wasn't comparable to this outer god Nyarlathotep, who was playing with dinosaurs millions of years ago.

Tyrannogod continued, "You see, in the time of the dinosaurs and even beforehand, there was a war on the Earth. Well, a series of wars spanning aeons. Several species came from the stars, flying on solar winds to call the Earth home. The most prolific of them, the elder things, erected cities of black stone. The worst, the star spawn, erected cities of green. Some would unite, and others would conquer. I am sure these places of loathsome green and black architecture still linger in the deep places of your world."

"The ruins I was in just then were mostly green stone," Randall wondered aloud.

"Yes, those ruins I found you by are linked to the Earth. It was called *the city that fell from the stars*. A poetic title for a dreadful place. Its true name, back in my time, was R'lyeh. Only it didn't fall from the stars. It was ripped from the Dark World and transplanted to the Earth when a conquering army arrived. Those ruins were the outer edges of that very same city. They just avoided the move across dimensions. In its time R'lyeh was home to both elder things and star spawn, depending on who conquered who."

Randall was suddenly filled with dread. He was certain he'd seen or heard the name R'lyeh before, though couldn't quite pin it in his memory. He knew that he'd never heard of aliens called the elder things before, nor the star spawn. It was fascinating to think that long before mankind, other beings had called the Earth home.

"That means the octopus men I saw were one of those two alien races..." Randall murmured.

"To have seen them and lived is an achievement," Tyrannogod stated, evidently impressed. "There are no elder things here, which means you encountered the original inhabitants of R'lyeh, the star spawn. I have heard rumours that some were trapped out here long ago."

"So, that city was here, this Dark World, then, in your time, it was pulled from here to the Earth?" Randall asked, trying to summarise the history of R'lyeh.

"It was well before my time," Tyrannogod answered. "Ancient beyond ancient is the great and terrible city of R'lyeh, home to the great dreamer..."

"Continue on with your story," Randall coaxed, desperate for more information. He couldn't believe that he was talking to a dinosaur about aliens.

"Of course," Tyrannogod said brightly. "Yes, I was but a beast, oblivious to the physical and divine wars around me. The elder things sometimes used us as beasts of burden while the star spawn hunted us for fun. I fell into a trap and roared the way a captured animal does. In my pain and fear, I was unlucky enough to catch the gaze of the crawling chaos, Nyarlathotep. He used the magic of his kind, the outer gods, to infect me. Eldritch magic, we call it, and it is cursed! I was given life eternal and intelligence like a natural being of the Earth had never had."

"It doesn't sound so bad..." Randall started hesitantly.

"Nyarlathotep is malevolent. He has many forms, manifesting as a friend or a traveller. Or, sometimes, as a towering tentacled monster. He knew that in giving me these gifts, I would be broken in my loneliness. Can you imagine having the desire to talk and not another soul that could understand... He named me the Dinosaur King, the leader of a doomed race of simple animals! The day the sky lit up with falling stars was when I felt peace. I could feel the great destruction approaching from the night sky..."

The meteor that killed the dinosaurs, Randall thought.

"Not even I could live through the ending of my kind. But at the last moment, when I stood before a shockwave of unimaginable proportion beneath a sky set ablaze with fire, Nyarlathotep appeared and opened a portal. He thrust me through it, and ever since, I have lingered here."

Randall felt the great lizard's despair as his words hung in the air. He wondered if that meant the dinosaur had been here for millions of years, or if time even worked the same in this

47

place. Regardless of the eternal despair of the T-Rex, Randall was grateful the dinosaur had appeared when he did.

"This Nyarlathotep, who you called an outer god... is he always on Earth? If he isn't a god of Earth, why was he there?" Randall asked Tyrannogod.

"If I could understand the machinations of the outer gods, I wouldn't be here. Nyarlathotep visits Earth from time to time as he crawls across the stars, sowing seeds of chaos... bringing with him his ill will..."

"What about the aliens you mentioned? Who built the cities of black stone? Couldn't you communicate with those elder things?" Randall asked, abruptly moving on from trying to understand the motives of the outer god.

Tyrannogod let out a deep thudding laugh.

"The elder things are more like plants than lifeforms like us. They communicate through a series of high-pitched musical notes. Not even eldritch magic bridges that gap."

"Oh, right," Randall mumbled.

"What is your story?" Tyrannogod asked him in turn.

Randall mumbled, "I am a scientist in training back home. I got wrapped up in a series of events I don't fully understand and here I am."

There was a particularly bright flash from above that ignited the treetops.

"Say, Tyrannogod, what are the strange lights in the sky?"

"As a scientist, you may be able to fathom what they are better than most. To put it in a biological context, they are similar to nerve cells that light up when an electrical signal passes through them."

"Nerve cells belonging to what exactly?" Randall said, aghast. The creature they belonged to must be enormous and, more frighteningly, all around them.

"Yog-Sothoth," Tyrannogod answered. Randall noted the contempt in his voice mirrored that when he mentioned Nyarlathotep.

"And Yog-Sothoth is another one of these outer gods?" Randall deduced.

"Yes. He is a multi-dimensional creature that we cannot properly comprehend. As old as the universe and more powerful than all things that ever were and ever will be, save one."

"A multi-dimensional creature..." Randall thought. Right away he knew there would be perception issues. It made sense that he'd be seeing random parts of the ancient god as lights in the sky because a three-dimensional creature like himself couldn't perceive higher realities. Any beings like Yog-Sothoth would appear disjointed, broken and horrific to his eyes.

"The old stories say that first was Chaos, who birthed the outer gods and primordials into the early universe. Chaos is said to be the only being that rivals Yog-Sothoth. Chaos is also the one who banished Yog-Sothoth to this dimension outside the universe," Tyrannogod concluded.

"When you say we are outside the universe, what exactly do you mean?" Randall asked.

"Well, you know the universe as an ever-expanding oval in the nothingness of creation. We exist right on the outer walls of the universe, in a thin ring that runs the entire circumference of it. Yog-Sothoth is a titanic being of unknowable proportion that exists all through this ring. We are simultaneously within and around him. It is safe to say there is nothing in this dimension that isn't influenced by Yog."

"What about this planet, with dirt and trees and living things?" Randall, when he suspended his disbelief, could imagine planets like this existing as micro-organisms inside such a being.

"Much like the universe, there are planets out here. Some have been brought here in the games of Nyarlathotep and others were manifested by Yog-Sothoth himself. Remnants of civilisations all across the universe that have dabbled in eldritch magic are here."

"Can Yog-Sothoth ever leave here and enter the real universe?"

"No," Tyrannogod said darkly. "This is his prison. Eldritch magic allows fragments of Yog-Sothoth to enter the universe briefly, and his power can travel in small amounts through the barriers between dimensions, but he is stuck out here. You will never find another outer god willingly venture here, as they would find themselves similarly trapped."

"Right, so we have an outer god inside the universe called Nyarlathotep and an outer god outside the universe called Yog-Sothoth," Randall said, trying to take verbal note of what he was learning. "What is the relationship between the two?"

Tyrannogod shook his head, causing Randall to wobble on his precarious perch. "I don't know. The nature of the outer gods is something I greatly desire to learn, but the information is difficult to come across, even though we are with Yog-Sothoth in his entrapment."

"But we aren't trapped, are we?" Randall asked, thinking back to the machine in the ruins. Those creatures, the star spawn, were clearly trying to get to the Earth. It seemed like they were close to achieving their goal.

"I have known those who have escaped. As I said, eldritch magic pulls monsters from this realm through the barrier all the time. There is no reason why you can't pass back through, should you find a way. And in ancient times, the entire city of R'lyeh was ripped from here."

A wave of determination hit Randall. Assuming the star spawn could get their portal device operational, he could escape the Dark World. He'd gotten in and out once. Surely, he could do it again.

A memory came rushing back to Randall. When he and Malcolm Selleck had been deciphering the coordinates in the Necronomicon, he was sure Malcolm had written down the word R'lyeh. It must've been mentioned in or around the passage they'd worked on! But then, did that mean... Had Randall unknowingly sent the Australian team to ruins containing an army of octopus monsters? It all made sense. An ancient city transplanted to the Earth, deep beneath the ocean... Randall had sent the Australian team to R'lyeh!

"What exactly are those things in the ruins? The star spawn monsters?" Randall asked urgently.

Tyrannogod's mood seemed to darken again as he spoke. "They are the soldiers of a great and terrible being named Cthulhu. Those outer ruins have always been rumoured to hold many of Cthulhu's army, accidentally left behind, forever waiting for their master's call."

"They are waking up. I saw them trying to activate a portal to Earth! Why would that be?"

"Hmm, that has not happened since I have been here. A very, very long time," Tyrannogod murmured. "I guess it can only mean one thing. Dread Lord Cthulhu is awake again. No one on Earth is safe."

"And Cthulhu is what exactly? A warlord or king of the star spawn?" Randall questioned. This was disturbing news. Could the Australian team have found the ruins and woken this being up?"

"Cthulhu is a great old one, a lesser being in the order of the outer gods. While he is nothing to Nyarlathotep or Yog-Sothoth, Cthulhu is still a calamity in his own right. In the ancient past, before even the dinosaurs, Cthulhu and his star spawn made war on the elder things and Earth's primordial deities. He is a conqueror, and from his city of R'lyeh, he will conquer."

That was an ominous thought. Cthulhu was obviously more than just an alien king if he made war on primordial deities. This sounded like a divine-level foe beyond the power of small gods like Artemis.

"Thank you, Tyrannogod. I think you have highlighted the urgency of the situation back on Earth. I need to get back and warn them. There is an army waiting in R'lyeh ready to attack!"

"If you desire to return to the Earth, there will be someone at our destination who can help you."

"Where is it that we are going?"

"The Village of the Lost."

CHAPTER 5

THE VILLAGE OF THE LOST

The rhythmic pounding of Tyrannogod's heavy steps stopped. Randall wiped his tired eyes and blinked several times in quick succession. He was faced with another new sight. A fortified wooden wall blocked the way.

Standing atop it were two of the horrific wailers from the fleshy forest. Their vacant bulging eyes gazed blindly out into the trees. They were partly obscured by the sets of long sloping armour haphazardly attached to their bodies, which had clearly been designed for much taller and differently shaped creatures. Randall's eyes travelled from the armour to the chains wrapping their torsos and fixing them to the top of the wall.

"They make useful guards," Tyrannogod answered Randall's unasked question.

Randall watched the two ghastly white monsters sway back and forth in their heavy chains, barely moving. He failed to deduce their usefulness from their presentation atop the wall.

There was the sound of wood scraping on dirt as the wall opened up before them. Two large doors were being dragged inwards.

Tyrannogod leaned forward, causing Randall to slide along the dinosaur's head and plop into the dirt.

"Forgive me, but I find it rather embarrassing to have another sentient creature riding me."

Randall brushed himself off. Now at ground level, the impressive fortifications towered over him. A serpentine, long-armed humanoid appeared through the open door, nodded curtly at the T-Rex and looked Randall up and down. Its small squinting eyes gave Randall an appraising look, before turning around and walking away.

"Was that an alien?" Randall asked.

"Alien is a bit of a derogatory term," Tyrannogod said quietly. "It implies not belonging, and we are all equal in the Village of the Lost."

Randall privately thought that was a bit of a stretch, but kept his mouth shut. He followed the dinosaur into the village.

It wasn't at all what he expected. Most of the buildings were large tepee-like structures with smoke billowing from them. A small rocky mound in the centre of the village contained a wide-open mouth. In stark contrast with the primitive façade were metal channels running across the ground carrying streams of glowing energy into each building. Each channel emanated from a hexagonal prism standing upright near the largest tepee and filled the air with a steaming gaseous cloud.

"Tyrannogod!" a raspy voice cried.

Randall was stunned. If the comically-named Dinosaur King had been odd, it had nothing on this creature.

Sliding towards them was a great yellow slug. The area that Randall determined to be the slimy animal's head featured two robotic stalks containing swivelling eyes and protruding fangs coming from its mouth. Atop the slug's back was a colossal brown shell.

It was a gigantic, vampiric, talking, cyborg snail. Though it wasn't a snail in the traditional sense as it had two thick gelatinous arms, each with a mechanical hand grafted on. At the end of each finger were what appeared to be small missiles.

"War Snail," the dinosaur boomed. "And Shwang!"

Randall was so fixated on the snail he hadn't even noticed the slug's companion. Walking beside it was another oddity. The being named Shwang was a human-swan hybrid. It had the torso of a man with the long sloping neck of a white swan. Randall suppressed a scoff when he saw that above its large flat bill was a red bandana. The swan-man didn't have wings springing from its back, instead, long feathers grew from its forearms. It looked completely incapable of flying.

Randall pinched himself. Surely, he was dreaming.

Yet, he didn't wake up.

He was still standing beside a dinosaur watching the snail and swan-man approach. This was not the life of a physicist. He dealt in hard science, not this cartoonish nonsense.

"Who is your companion?" War Snail asked, his spinning eyes locking on to Randall.

"Randall Dare, a new arrival in the Dark World," Tyrannogod answered.

Randall extended a hand for the snail to shake, then quickly retracted the offer. He didn't want to touch its missile fingers.

"Oh yes, the blip we detected. Good to see you survived in the forest. The village may look primitive but we have some advanced technology here that helps us in our goals," War Snail explained excitedly.

"Your name isn't really War Snail though, is it?" Randall hoped he wasn't being rude, but again he felt like he was in a child's imagination.

"My true name is a sequence of complex numbers that is difficult to state. I was given the name War Snail as a mark of endearment from a traveller. He seemed to find it fitting so I accepted it."

"Are you from the Earth?" Randall asked.

"No," War Snail answered.

Shwang squawked loudly.

"Why can I understand you?"

"Because Yog-Sothoth can understand you. All things in his realm are influenced by him and thus can communicate with each other."

"Right."

War Snail looked up at Tryannogod. "It is usual to have one being from one world here. Yet now three of these small pink apes are in our immediate vicinity. Spells trouble to me."

"There are two other humans here?" Randall interjected quickly.

"Yes. I will take you to a place you can rest. Then, when you awaken, I will arrange for you to speak with Carter. He's been in the village for about fifty Earth years."

"Carter!" Randall thought. There was a man here named Carter.

"Who is the other?" he asked excitedly.

"Don't know his name. Not sure he is entirely human, to be honest," Tyrannogod murmured. "He lives away from the village. Wanders through the trees wearing a long cloak and hood. The traveller, we call him…"

Shwang, the swan-man, now spoke up, speaking in a high-pitched tone that sounded as ridiculous as he looked. "Very few safe paths here. Not wise to wander alone."

"Is the whole planet like this?" Randall asked, looking up towards the pulsing lights in the sky.

"What do you mean?" War Snail questioned.

"Just spooky forests, ruins and scattered villages like this?"

"No. The Dark World is incredibly diverse. There are places with sunrises and sunsets across twisting seas. All artificial or designed by magic, mind you. There are kingdoms of glass and huge floating islands. Go north from here and you enter the lands ruled by the Twelve Lords of the Nevernight. Go east and find yourself in the grip of the Fourteen Kings of the Carn and the Wars of Forasythis. Moonships piloted by fell queens travel through the void to lands of dreams. There are great stories that come from the Dark World."

"Then why are you all here? In this gloomy place where wailers wander the forests?" Randall asked sincerely. It sounded like if he left the immediate vicinity, he could get wrapped in a fantastical adventure with knights and princesses.

War Snail sent a sideward glance to Tyrannogod, who proceeded as if Randall hadn't asked the question.

"Come now Randall, there is guest accommodation nearby. I could feel you slipping during the journey here. Sleep comes easily in the Dark World. We will arrange your own accommodation in the coming days."

Randall looked up into the dinosaur's cold reptilian eye. There was no comfort to be found there. He did desperately need to sleep, so wasn't going to argue about the abrupt end to the conversation.

"You will come to my home," Tyrannogod instructed, pointing his head towards the rocky mound in the centre of the village. "Don't worry, the larger cave structure is for me, but there are purpose-built lodgings for guests inside."

Randall was pleasantly surprised when he stepped into one of the lodgings. It had no roof, which was really his only complaint. Instead, the dark brown of the rocks above sat ominously overhead. Still, there was a simply made mattress with blankets and pillows that were surprisingly comfortable. It all looked hand stitched.

His last thought as he clambered onto the bed was that he would wake up back in Switzerland and realise this had all been a horrible dream. He hadn't spoken with a giant snail or a T-Rex. He'd never met Artemis or learned his brother was a werewolf. Yep, soon he'd wake up and everything would be normal again.

The second Randall's head touched the pillow, he left the

Dark World for the land of dreams.

• • • • •

"AAAAAHHHH!" RANDALL YELLED as he awoke to the sight of enormous jaws above him. In his sleep, he'd forgotten where he was. The octo-men, the wailers and the dinosaur came rushing back as consciousness gripped him again.

"Jesus Christ," Randall muttered as he got to his feet, his body pulsing with adrenaline.

"Didn't mean to disturb you," Tyrannogod said dismissively.

Disturb? Randall had just been scared half to death.

"That was very alarming," Randall stated, not trying to hide his annoyance.

"You have been asleep for a long time," Tyrannogod yawned.

Randall did feel a lot better.

"Why do you live here?" Randall asked at once. The lingering question from their last conversation rushed back to him.

"We will discuss that after you speak to Carter."

"But, I-"

"After you speak to Carter," Tyrannogod emphasised. There was a low growl in his voice that told Randall he shouldn't argue the point.

"Fine," Randall agreed reluctantly. He was desperately excited to speak to another person.

"He is up and awake too. I just checked."

"I'm happy to go when you are," Randall said, sliding his

sneakers onto his feet.

They left the cavern mouth and walked around the rocky mound. Another collection of tepees and primitive mud huts met them on the other side, all connected by the same channels of energy.

"What are these?" Randall indicated a nearby pipeline half-submerged in the ground.

"Some beings come here with devices that require a power source. These channels power everything. You saw the hexagonal prism on the other side?"

Randall did recall seeing the upright structure.

"That houses an artefact called the Stone of Ebiziad. Another thing cast away to the Dark World. A traveller once told us the stone's tale. A gallant hero fought the forces of evil to remove it from their world for all time, naming it too powerful for any mortal to possess. We aren't sure of its full capabilities, but it naturally generates power that can be harnessed."

Randall nodded, content with the answer. This place was like the mythological past, the present and the technological future had merged into one.

"Look to the sky," Tyrannogod instructed.

Randall tilted his head upwards and gasped in horror. Like an ominous cloud high above, sat a pulsating patch of torn flesh containing hundreds of eyes popping and sucking back into the depths of the blob.

On the far horizon, Randall saw building-sized tentacles reaching high into the sky.

"I assume that Yog-Sothoth has his attention focused

somewhere around here," Tyrannogod said, not at all sounding fussed about it.

"Can he see us?" Randall asked, panicked.

"Perhaps, but I doubt whatever has attracted his attention is perceivable to us anyway."

There was a prolonged slurping sound and the cloud of flesh and eyes faded from view.

Randall shuddered. This was a foreboding place.

Randall fell into one of Tyrannogod's large three-toed footprints.

"Carter," the dinosaur boomed, stopping just shy of one of the mud huts. The door creaked open and an old man emerged. Randall hastily tried to wipe the mud from his pants as he got to his feet. Upon closer inspection, 'old' didn't do him justice. The man was wretchedly ancient, covered in liver spots with barely a wisp of white hair. He did still maintain an impressively bushy moustache.

"ARGH! Tyrannogod, you scare me every time I see you!" Carter wheezed, clapping his hands to his chest.

The old man squinted up at the dinosaur, then shifted his gaze to Randall. It wasn't a particularly friendly look.

"Send word in the usual way, I will be in the library," Tyrannogod sighed, before turning around and thundering off.

"They have a library?" Randall asked himself aloud.

"Yes, my boy, yes. You dense or something? Skinny runt of a man," the old man mumbled.

Randall's excitement drained quickly. The only other human in the village was an old coot.

He held the rough wooden door open for Randall, though with some difficulty. Randall stepped into the simple home. It held a roaring fire, a chair, a simple dresser with six drawers and a bed. The man didn't have much in the way of worldly possessions.

"So, you're Carter," Randall started, looking around for somewhere to sit.

"Sit on the bed," Carter directed, hobbling over to his chair. "I'd offer you something to drink if I had anything. Tall fellow, aren't you? You remind me of my lazy no-good son, the useless shoe salesman..."

"Randall Dare," Randall offered to break the awkward pause.

"William Eisenhein Carter," the old-timer stated, his cloudy eyes lighting up with pride.

"That name sounds familiar," Randall thought. He felt like he'd heard it recently.

Randall looked at the man's clothes. He looked to be wearing an old-school safari suit that had been patched up a thousand times. Its long sleeves were muddy and discoloured.

"Do you know of my exploits?" Carter asked Randall.

"Ah, no," Randall answered honestly.

Carter looked crestfallen, though he quickly regained his composure. "Probably a good thing. Don't want to intimidate you now, do we? I was a renowned explorer in my time. Later in my life, I became an Egyptologist. Big discoveries, but all hush-hush. Really, they should teach about me in schools."

"Right," Randall smiled politely, unsure what to say.

"That blasted dinosaur told me what happened, you opening a portal and all. He'll eat us all one day when he reverts back to his primal state. But you, you survived a journey into the R'lyeh ruins too. That's impressive stuff."

"Thanks," Randall replied.

"How'd you open the portal to the Dark World?" Carter asked eagerly.

"The Necronomicon. It had an equation in it that I solved."

"Cursed book," Carter spat.

"You know it?" Randall didn't hide his surprise well.

"Of course I know it, boy! Are you a twit, or do you not know you're on an alien world?"

Randall rolled his eyes. Carter either didn't see or ignored him, choosing instead to tell his story.

"I encountered it during my second last adventure on Earth. It was 1958 when I was pulled out of retirement by an eager young entrepreneur named Achilles Aetos. Foolish man, wet behind the ears too. Never did make good choices. He was looking to make his fortune in Egypt and wanted an Egyptologist to help him find ruins in the desert.

"SANDSTORM!" Carter shouted, causing Randall to jump in fright. "Vicious sandstorm separated us. It took two days for rescuers to find us all out there. Blasted sand everywhere! Achilles was sheepish. I pressed him and concluded he'd found something, something he wanted to keep to himself. Before we went our separate ways, I snuck into his hotel room and found the object he so desired to hide from me. The black book, the Necronomicon…"

Carter's eyes glazed over as if he was lost in memory. Randall's copy of the Necronomicon had come from Amsterdam. It seemed unlikely that this was the same book.

"Did you solve the equation and end up here too?" Randall asked.

"No, my boy, no. I only had a few hours with the book, though I learned some of its history later. You see, I thought Achilles had found a treasure, not a book. But when I scanned through the pages, I saw something important. I saw drawings of cities, cities that I'd seen before. Black stone at concave and convex angles. Non-Euclidian geometry. Strange spheres and five-pointed stars...

"You see, my greatest adventure was in South America. Deep in the jungles, there were rumours of odd black stone structures at the base of a high plateau. No one had ever made it up to the plateau. I was young, ambitious and formed a team to do just that. What we found was a preserved world from a different age of the Earth. Dinosaurs, like Tyrannogod, only wild and free, co-existing with tribes of ape-men and primitive peoples. All over the plateau were the ruins of an ancient civilisation, a non-human civilisation. There was a link between the survival of that primeval world and the black stones, though it was beyond me at the time to figure it out."

Randall was taken aback at how William Carter spoke with the voice of a younger man as he recounted his adventures. It was certainly interesting, though didn't seem all too relevant to his current predicament.

Carter coughed violently before continuing, "Later in my life the United States Government sent me to Antarctica on a top-secret mission. There'd been a disaster there, you see. A research team had discovered black stone ruins in the mountains. Apparently, they'd awoken the creatures that had once dwelled there. Due to my experience in South America, they thought I'd be mentally and physically equipped to deal with whatever prehistoric threats may appear. When I was on the ancient plateau, I killed a flying pterosaur with a spear. Kept the spear and wing as a keepsake. Anyway, I knew right away that this mission was abnormal. Gone were the usual dreary scientists and military contractors; instead, I was introduced to members of a group called The Old World. Ghost hunters and chasers of the paranormal, or so I thought. Working with us also were representatives from the United States Supernatural Occurrence Taskforce, or USSOT."

Randall found this very intriguing. He was currently working with both The Old World and USSOT, though didn't know much about either organisation. Carter picked up on Randall's recognition.

"You know them. There is more to your coming here than your simple story tells," he said with an accusatory tone.

"Well, I was picked up by an Australian Government team that is working with both The Old World and USSOT," Randall shrugged. "I've only been a part of their mission for a few days. They seemed to think that a passage in the Necronomicon was indicating the location of the lost city of Atlantis. I helped translate the coordinates, and they went off to find it. I now think what they actually went to find was a city called R'lyeh."

Carter looked at Randall with a grim expression. His old eyes sparkled with thought.

"There was a man on my expedition… an odd fellow who went by the name Altior Fulgur. Not a care in the world despite the perilous circumstances we found ourselves in. He made several bold claims, claims I didn't believe until I had that Necronomicon in front of me so many years later. You see, we didn't just find ruins in Antarctica, we found a megastructure buried under the ice. We explored the structure and found statues and murals. Altior worked to collect photographic evidence and compile the story the city told. Elder things flew across the stars to the Earth and built cities of black stone. But in those cities were artefacts made of a different type of material. Statuettes depicted an octopus-headed god of sorts, always carved in green soapstone. Sometimes, the cities of black had building-sized shrines dedicated to the creature.

"Altior claimed that the creature depicted was not one of the elder things. It was a different kind of being. A god-like alien who commanded an army that made war on the elder things in the lost aeons of history."

"Cthulhu and the star spawn," Randall chimed in. "Tyrannogod told me about them on the way here. They are active in the ruins."

"Yes, Cthulhu… I had heard this name before, as a young man. Everyone on Earth knows the name in their subconscious. The great dreamer… In his long slumber, all life has felt his influence like a faint flicker inside their minds. The more susceptible go mad and get locked up. And some find each other. As old as humanity is the dark and terrible Cult of Cthulhu, humans who worship this singular beacon of destruction. To them, the Necronomicon is like a bible.

"It is easy for me to believe now, but at the time the idea of alien gods and wars from millions of years ago was preposterous, even with all I'd seen. Altior even went as far as to say that the sunken city of Cthulhu was larger than the one we'd found in Antarctica. He wanted to find it. There was a thirst about him... a great desire to see R'lyeh. He said it would be similar in appearance to our findings in Antarctica, though far larger, with green stone architecture. Altior claimed, based on what he'd seen, that over thousands of years, the cultures of the elder things and star spawn had blended. R'lyeh, if found, would be a city of green and black stone of colossal proportion, holding the knowledge of the two races that had occupied it."

"None of Altior's predictions seem absurd, considering the subject matter," Randall chimed in.

"You're right, of course," Carter replied. "Where he lost me was in his claims about Cthulhu's nature. I hate to use words like *magical*, but it was Altior who insisted that Cthulhu wasn't an ordinary being. He was divine. He was *magical*. So, I asked him, 'how did the elder things, who according to the history we saw, beat Cthulhu if they were biological creatures?'. Altior's answer was that the elder things had divine help from Earth's early gods. Primordial beings like Gaia, Tartarus and Ouranos teamed up with the elder things to fight Cthulhu.

"I always considered that suggestion outrageous. But then, as I flicked through Achilles Aetos' book, I saw it. Images of Earth's primordials sending Cthulhu into a deep slumber. Altior Fulgur's claims were here, written down for all to see! But how had he known? Then it struck me that Altior must've read the Necronomicon before our expedition to Antarctica. He was the most willing to accept a story about elder things and star spawn because he'd read it all before.

"I wanted a copy of the book to read for my own, so I contacted The Old World in Europe, then in the USA, and then in Japan. None of their branch heads had ever heard of the Necronomicon. If they were all lying to me, they were very convincing. Further to that, none of them were willing to speak to me about Altior Fulgur. I assumed him to be dead, as he'd already been getting on when we were in Antarctica. The man had wanted to find R'lyeh. I recall him saying that wherever the city was there'd be unusual life around it. Large and ancient creatures…"

Randall's mind jumped to giant squid. The New Zealand company that had agreed to take the Australian team to R'lyeh had been noticed by someone connected to The Old World because they'd discovered a new species of giant squid. Randall wished he'd been privy to the details. He cursed himself for not asking more questions or paying closer attention to what the Australian team were doing.

But something occurred to Randall that didn't make sense.

"I found the coordinates to, what I suspect at least, is R'lyeh in the Necronomicon. If Altior had knowledge of the book, wouldn't he also have known where to find R'lyeh?"

"BAH! There are any number of reasons why he would not have known. Perhaps the knowledge to decode the passage was not available when he had the book? Or he chose to ignore a complex alien code for the sake of laziness. Your guess as to why is as good as mine, but I am certain of two things: Altior was familiar with the Necronomicon and he didn't know the location of R'lyeh."

"Did he have a reason for wanting to find R'lyeh so badly?" Randall asked.

"No. There was more to the man than he let on," Carter answered.

"Let me see if I understand this right. We potentially have Cthulhu on Earth, who is a god-like alien warlord of extreme power. He is a lesser version of an outer god, like Yog-Sothoth, who is just a large bunch of eyes floating out there in the abyss."

Carter seemed to take personal offence at the simplicity of Randall's summary.

"No, no, my boy! Yog-Sothoth is more than some dark being floating out in the abyss. He is both the key and the gate! He is unfathomable!"

"The key and gate?" Randall questioned. "Isn't he trapped out here?"

"Not a physical key and gate. He is the very concept of knowledge itself. He is not trapped. We may perceive it as some barrier dimension on the edge of reality, but the true nature of this realm is as a cosmic throne from which Yog exists as time and space!"

William suddenly looked weary. He wiped the sweat from his brow and slumped back in his chair.

"Tyrannogod is under the assumption, misguided as it may be, that because I am human, I will have an easier time judging your intentions," Carter said after a moment. "He does not wish for spies of Nyarlathotep in the village. I think it is plain that you are no spy. I will send him word."

"Why are they here? Tyrannogod, War Snail and the others?" Randall asked.

"This village sits on an ancient repository of knowledge that has been collected over the life of the universe. Tyrannogod and those like him have a singular mind directed towards one purpose, learning how to harm an outer god."

Randall was confused. So far, it had sounded like the outer gods were immortal and invincible.

"They understand that Yog-Sothoth is out of reach. They all seek revenge against Nyarlathotep. Because Nyarlathotep plays his tricks and speaks with mortals, they perceive him as lesser and potentially vulnerable, but they are wrong. I may have only scratched the surface of eldritch knowledge, but I am certain that Nyarlathotep is beyond any of them," Carter sighed.

"It doesn't make sense to me. I would think that if these creatures existed as part of our universe, then no matter how powerful, something would act as an opposite force to them. They should be able to be destroyed," Randall said.

"The nature of the outer gods is the subject of much debate here. There are ways to communicate with the outer gods. Even Yog-Sothoth can present himself to mortal beings, though he can never truly speak with us. I imagine it would be like walking into a cloud of knowledge that hung as mist in the air. Your mind would perceive and grasp what it could at random as you walked through, but the information would be subject to your own interpretation and understanding."

"Has their research yielded any results?" Randall asked, hopeful. It occurred to him that even though they hadn't found a way to hurt an outer god, they may still have information to help in the coming fight against Cthulhu and his star spawn.

"No, not yet. So, they continue their eternal search. It has been a pleasure talking with you, Randall Dare, but I am dreadfully tired now. We will talk again soon, I'm sure."

Randall stood up and thanked the old man. He strode out of the mud hut with more questions than when he'd entered. On a more positive note, he now also had an idea of what he needed to do.

First, he needed to learn about the library hidden somewhere in this village. There was no way that this place full of aliens and monsters didn't have a copy of the Necronomicon. Randall suspected that the equation that got him here may be all the star spawn needed to get their portal working in the ruins. Plus, if Tyrannogod and War Snail were looking for methods of harming an outer god, they may have dredged up information on R'lyeh and Cthulhu. He needed to get whatever information he could on Cthulhu's weaknesses to help the team back on Earth. Then he could make a plan to get back to Earth.

It was time for a frank discussion with Tyrannogod.

Fortunately, the dinosaur was easy to find. His great clomping footsteps shook the ground as he moved.

"Tyrannogod!" Randall called, running towards the T-Rex.

"Randall Dare. I have already received word from Carter that he does not believe you to be a spy of Nyarlathotep."

"No, I'd never even heard of him before. And to be honest, it's not really him I have an interest in, I'd rather learn about Cthulhu."

"The great old ones are lesser calamities than the outer gods, so they haven't absorbed much of our research. Nevertheless, you are free to peruse the library at your leisure."

"Where is this library?"

"Below us," Tyrannogod grinned. "Come with me. You'll find this fascinating."

Randall jogged to keep up with Tyrannogod as he thundered around the perimeter of the village. They passed collections of stone castle-like structures that Randall hadn't seen before. All sorts of creatures peeked out at the odd pair as they passed.

A good night's sleep had done wonders for Randall's nerves. He felt refreshed and far more accepting of his new life circumstances. He had to embrace the ridiculousness of it all just to get through it. A small smile crossed his face as he travelled in the shadow of the fearsome dinosaur. At this moment, Randall Dare was truly alive and capable of anything. There was knowledge beyond anything he could learn through conventional means here, and he was going to seize the opportunity.

They soon came to the tall perimeter wall, though this portion was coated in a thick mass of purple vines. They looked poisonous.

Tyrannogod stamped hard on the ground. The sound of squeaky gears spinning to life was followed by prolonged metallic mourning as a huge portion of earth slid away.

Roughly hewn stairs descended into the darkness of the

newly revealed cavern.

"Simply touch the black cube and the door will open," Tyrannogod instructed as he stepped aside.

Randall saw a small black cube half buried in the dirt where Tyrannogod had stepped. It glowed with deathly energy, making Randall privately doubt the idea of pointing his fingers anywhere near it.

"It is fine, it just looks dangerous because of the sheer mass of energy flowing down here," Tyrannogod stated, dismissive of Randall's concerned features.

"Why did you build the library so far away from the village centre?" Randall asked.

"We did not build this place. This is a manifestation of the Dark World."

Tyrannogod awkwardly began his journey down the stairs. While the hole in the ground was wide enough for him, his feet were too large for the steps.

The darkness abated quickly as a serene blue glow engulfed the underground tunnel. They came to a small bridge crossing the most fantastic river Randall had ever seen. It was like a torrent of blue plasma coursing at incredible speeds through a deep channel in the ground. Small pockets of red and green whizzed by in the stream.

"What is this?" Randall breathed.

"Knowledge," Tyrannogod answered as they crossed the bridge.

Randall wanted to dip his hand into the current and let the transfixing energy wash over it. It looked so inviting to the touch.

Yet, there was something of a warning in the swirling colours below. Randall decided he wouldn't touch anything unless explicitly told it was safe.

They came through a high arch into a room supported by tall columns. The light of the river ignited the enormous cavern in a blaze of colour. On all sides were towering piles of books.

"What do you see?" Tyrannogod asked.

"Books," Randall answered, struggling to comprehend the sheer amount of them.

"Funny how that works," a raspy voice said from behind a column. War Snail glided into view.

"To me, we are surrounded by computer terminals outputting raw data on their screens."

"Why do we perceive it differently?" Randall asked. There were certainly no computers in the immediate vicinity.

"That is how the nexus works. Go to the end of the hall and you will see it."

Randall continued forward among the immense volumes of knowledge all around. The light got brighter the deeper he journeyed into the room.

He came to a silver door decorated with disturbing art. Bubbling eyes and tentacles were etched with fine detail on its surface. The artist had drawn the fragmented visage of Yog-Sothoth.

Randall looked back at Tyrannogod, who nodded his enormous head encouragingly. Randall pushed the door open and gasped.

Before him, floating in mid-air in another colossal room, was a blue star. It was intensely bright, yet didn't hurt his eyes to look at. Energy flowed from the fiery sphere in several thick streams, disappearing into channels in the rock walls.

There was a series of small mechanical clicks as War Snail slid up beside Randall. One eye stalk turned towards the human, while the other remained locked on the star.

"While the information look different to every creature that comes down here, this always looks the same. Much like the lights high above the Dark World, we are looking at part of Yog-Sothoth. A small fragment of his mind, I think. You can see his thoughts manifesting as raw power."

"William Carter told me that Yog-Sothoth 'was knowledge'. Is this what he was talking about?" Randall asked.

"That is his interpretation of the outer god, and he may be right. We just don't know."

Randall ripped his gaze from the magnificent star and turned to War Snail. "How am I meant to search this library?"

"With these!" War Snail clicked his fingers and a procession of small objects came zooming towards them. Randall instinctively ducked. Then, after feeling cowardly and stupid, Randall observed the buzzing things closely. They were clearly a kind of advanced drone.

"They have gravity pads on them. You simply tell the device what you are looking for, and it will scan the surroundings for matching words and themes. We have several dozen drones, and I don't mind setting aside a couple for your use. After all, who knows how long you will be with us."

"Easy as that, hey?" Randall marvelled. "Surely you should've found everything you need by now?"

"Well, my understanding of this cavern isn't as complete as I'd like. We know that the information here exists. As in, it's not created by individuals entering the space. We just perceive it in the way that is most comfortable to us. It also appears that what can be found here is limited in scope, though we come across new information every day. Random knowledge from the physical universe appears here with no discernible pattern or reason. And, it appears in such huge quantities that sorting through it is a monumental task," War Snail explained.

"I suspect that because fragments of Yog-Sothoth are frequently being summoned, or small parts of him are constantly breaking into the universe, that knowledge attaches to him like a cosmic parasite. Those parasites then get deposited here," Tyrannogod speculated.

"Right, and this nexus... what happens if you touch it?" Randall asked. The allure of it was so strong he felt like a moth to a flame, desperate to immerse himself in the energy.

"What do you imagine happens when beings place themselves directly into Yog-Sothoth's thoughts?" Tyrannogod replied coldly.

"He sees you," Randall responded. "I imagine that for one small moment, Yog-Sothoth's attention diverts entirely to you."

"And, in that moment, you are destroyed," War Snail concluded.

"It would have to be the most incredible of circumstances for a living soul to survive that encounter. Only a being with a destiny that Yog-Sothoth wants to indulge in could live. That is my theory," Tyrannogod added.

"I have a theory about that energy, too," War Snail chimed in excitedly. "We all carry the scars of our foolish interactions with eldritch magic."

Randall looked at the green patch on Tyrannogod's head with its extra eyes and tentacles.

"I think that if you were to throw yourself into the energy stream and survive, it is the only way to experience eldritch magic without being corrupted by it. What benefit that would achieve, I don't know. But I'm sure there are applications for such a power," War Snail continued.

"Leave such thoughts behind," Tyrannogod said to Randall. "In these halls of vast knowledge, we hope to find the undoing of the outer gods. If you so desire, you are welcome to join us in our quest."

"Yes," Randall nodded. "Though, as I said, there is information I want to find as well. For my own purposes."

"Then there is no time like the present to start. Here, I will teach you how to use the drones," War Snail said.

Randall took one last look at the nexus before turning away. Deep down, some part of him knew that the glowing star had a role to play in this adventure yet. He could feel it in his bones, which was odd. As a man of science, he'd never paid much heed to emotions and superstition.

Randall chuckled as he tuned into the large gelatinous slug's explanation of how to work the drones.

CHAPTER 6

NEANDERTHAL

There was no way to tell the passing of time. Randall slept whenever he felt like sleeping and spent the rest of his time in the underground library. Trying to sift through the books was an almost impossible task, even with the aid of the drones. If it wasn't for War Snail's cybernetic implants and personal assistance, Randall wouldn't have been able to find a place to start.

It was a pleasant side effect of the Dark World that many of the alien books translated into English as soon as he opened them. When Randall, at last, located a copy of the Necronomicon, he was ecstatic. The entire book, with all its horrible secrets, was his to enjoy in plain old English. The macabre imagery remained the same, causing Randall to skip over certain portions where the illustrations were just too grotesque.

He quickly found the equation that had brought him here

and set about resolving it. He drew the entire thing out in the dirt and braced for a portal to open. He'd mentally prepared for the possibility that the equation was a one-way ticket to the Dark World, but it was disappointing nonetheless when nothing happened. Still, Randall set to work memorising the whole thing. He couldn't shake the suspicion that this equation would come into play eventually. There was also the monumental task of trying to reverse-engineer it and discover exactly what the equation meant. It was complex beyond belief, but that didn't mean that understanding it was an insurmountable task. He was sure the key to opening the door the other way was hidden in the numbers.

The rest of the Necronomicon was interesting, though it read as if someone had just hobbled together disjointed passages from contradictory books. Some pages detailed the complex histories of the great old ones on Earth, and others contained spells and incantations along with their associated rituals. Much to Randall's surprise, the book didn't shy away from discussing Earth's gods. He found the section detailing the missing power of Zeus and how to claim it, though the whole thing was written in past tense and read more like a story with incidental instructions on how to take the power. Without its alien language, the book lost a lot of its eeriness. Randall even began to think that the whole thing was rather badly written.

After what he figured was the better part of a week, his initial captivation with the Necronomicon ceased and Randall began to assist the other denizens of the village in trying to find books that talked about the outer gods. An impressive collection of tomes had already been dissected and analysed, with little useful information on combatting the outer gods found. It left Randall with the impression that the outer gods were invulnerable in almost every way. It was like they just didn't belong in the universe.

Adjustment to life in the Village of the Lost was easy. Food came in the form of strange meats hunted in the forest. Tyrannogod would lumber in holding the carcasses of unknown beasts, which would then be carved up and cooked on spits. The all-meat diet was beginning to wreak havoc on Randall's digestive system. Water was collected from a nearby stream, though Randall hated his turns to drag the heavy buckets to and from the crystal pools. He sometimes heard wailers in the distance, screaming and shrieking in the dim light. The only true culture shock came from the variety of sentient species that called the village home. Many were bipedal and humanoid, though some existed as forms of light or clouds of gas. Despite the magic of Yog-Sothoth linking all things in the Dark World, Randall still found he couldn't speak with some of the odder species.

Much to Randall's annoyance, none of the inhabitants of the village wanted to discuss his escape plan. They were adamant that returning to the ruins of R'lyeh was a suicide mission and wouldn't indulge in his fantasies at all. He'd identified the problems he'd need to hurdle in the order they would require solving. First was knowing how to fix the star spawn's portal machine, which he was working on. He hoped the answer to that was reverse engineering the equation that got him here. The next was being able to use the alien's tech. Randall would have to use the control pad to input the numbers he wanted, which meant it would have to respond to him. The third was getting into the portal room, though this was the easiest point to address, as he was sure the star spawn would've fixed the teleport pad he'd escaped through.

Hope flashed in Randall like the pulsing of the squashed ovals above. He just needed some allies in his quest. Every day that passed in the gloom of the Dark World grew Randall's confidence. He was beginning to feel a twinge of destiny being in this place. The mysterious machinations of aliens and gods had brought him here, and he was starting to feel like he could play his role.

• • • • •

ON ONE PARTICULARLY DARK and dreary morning, Randall's feet were sinking into the soft earth as he walked hunched across the village. He'd just completed a rather unpleasant bowel movement and his stomach didn't feel quite right. How he longed to eat something green for once.

"SHREEEEEEEEEEE!"

The sound cut through the air like a hot knife in butter.

It wasn't a sound Randall had heard here before. It sounded like a shrill, pained scream coming from the forest.

The ground shook beneath rapidly approaching heavy footsteps.

"Open the gate!" Tyrannogod roared as he thundered past Randall.

"What is it?" Randall called.

"An eldritch beast is here," the dinosaur grumbled as he passed through the divide into the forest.

"Eldritch beast?" Randall asked no one. Evidently, this was a serious problem, as the entire village had spurred into a flurry of activity. Several of the aliens were throwing on armour plates and equipping themselves with primitive weapons.

The horrific wail carried across the open ground again, causing the hair on the back of Randall's neck to stand up.

"What is going on?" Randall asked a reptilian bug-eyed creature as it scurried past.

"We defend the inner walls," it hissed back.

"Isn't anyone going to help Tyrannogod?"

"No, his size and raw strength are his weapons. If the monster gets through him, we can only hope to defend the village and drive it away."

Randall looked towards the open gate and gulped. He couldn't let Tyrannogod face this new danger alone, could he? But then, what could he do?

"I'm not a coward!" Randall yelled at himself, causing the alien to jump. He whipped the simple wooden spear from the alien's webbed hand and turned toward the swiftly closing gate. The wailers on top seemed particularly agitated as they struggled against their binding chains.

Caught in the grip of temporary insanity, Randall dived through the gate and was confronted with the dreadful gloom of the forest. Fortunately, there was a set of large three-toed footprints for him to follow. There was something else too... a smell hung in the air that was so repulsive it almost caused Randall to throw up just from breathing it in. The odour was otherworldly in its perversion.

A booming roar shook the trees from nearby. It was met with a shrill wail. Tyrannogod had found his target.

Randall mustered his courage and ran. A swirling mix of thrill and dread clouded his brain. What was he doing, running into the forest like this? Had he gone mad?

He hopped roots and pushed through vines until he came to the site of the battle.

Head down, like a charging bull, Tyrannogod slammed into the eldritch beast, causing it to reel up. Randall was stopped in his tracks by the creature's appearance. It was a conical wall of flesh on four thin legs. It was taller than the T-Rex with no recognisable body parts. It was a mound of eyes, oozing orifices and female breasts, with huge grey tentacles springing from its body at random. They flailed wildly, ripping branches from the trees and tearing huge gashes in the dirt.

The eldritch beast absorbed the dinosaur's blow with ease, wrapping two of its thick tentacles around Tyrannogod's head and neck.

"No!" Randall yelled, seeing the spine-breaking twist before it happened.

Randall dived into the clearing and thrust his wooden spear into one of the eldritch monster's eyeballs. It spun on its hooves and released Tyrannogod just in the nick of time.

"Oh god," Randall uttered as thick grey tentacles wrapped around him tightly. He spluttered as the air was squeezed from his lungs. The spear in his hand snapped as Randall was hoisted into the air, his eyeballs bulging and the taste of blood filling his mouth.

Tyrannogod roared and lunged again, his enormous teeth sinking into the side of the monster. It squealed and dropped Randall, who collapsed in agony. He coughed violently, coating the dirt in globs of blood. He was sure several of his ribs were broken.

Dust flew as Randall rolled away from the monster's hooves in a series of agonising heaves.

"Over here!" a voice croaked.

Randall looked up and saw a man lying against the base of a nearby tree. Randall pulled himself through the mud towards the stranger, almost blacking out with each pained movement.

The stranger was dressed in black military attire, with damaged body armour hanging from his webbing. He had a handgun on his right hip and several ammo pouches on his left. A rifle was still slung around his neck, though it sat in the dirt beside him. He had short brown hair, a square jaw and blood dribbling down his chin.

"Randall Dare," the man smiled weakly.

"Who are you?" Randall said, taken aback.

"Neanderthal," he spluttered. "I know your brother. The family resemblance is unmistakable."

"Josh or Kane?" Randall asked.

"Both, actually."

There was a huge crash as Tyrannogod was hoisted from the ground and body-slammed into a tree, smashing it. The dinosaur groaned loudly as he tried to roll.

"Can you throw?" Neanderthal asked Randall.

"Yeah," Randall answered.

"My arms are broken. Take one of the incendiary grenades from my belt, the ones with the symbol of fire on them, pull the pin and throw it at the monster. It was pretty effective before."

Randall did as instructed, forcing himself upright with great difficulty. He felt the cool metal shell of the grenade in his hand as he fumbled to remove it from the soldier's belt. He pulled the pin and threw it at the eldritch beast, which was quickly engulfed in flame.

This gave Tyrannogod the seconds he needed to shake himself off and get back into the fight.

"How else can I help?" Randall asked Neanderthal.

"Take my rifle."

With sharp breaths, Randall groaned to his feet and unslung the rifle from Neanderthal. He pointed it at the flaming monstrosity, now squealing as it ambled back and forth. Like a shark, Tyrannogod menacingly circled it, waiting for a moment to strike.

"No," Neanderthal croaked. "Not for that, for the professor..."

"What?"

The wind was knocked out of Randall as a purple blur whipped him from his feet. The pain made him woozy.

Standing over him was a familiar, but mangled face. It was Malcolm Selleck! He was the professor Randall had translated part of the Necronomicon with. Only, something dreadful had happened to him. Half of his head was purple, with one eye grotesquely enlarged, popping from his skull. His right arm had been replaced with a powerful tentacle and his right leg was engorged, all of it purple and stinking.

"Professor Selleck," Randall breathed.

The professor just gurgled and shook his head, spraying Randall with salivary foam.

Tyrannogod lifted the eldritch beast off its cloven feet and toppled the conical mound of eyes and breasts.

The professor wrapped his tentacle arm around Randall's neck. Randall clawed at the tentacle as he struggled for air, but there was nothing he could do.

"Release him," a serene voice commanded. A shockwave rippled through the clearing as the mutated academic was blasted back. The tentacle released and Randall sucked in welcomed breaths of air.

Randall suddenly felt light as a feather as he glowed with an unfamiliar energy. He turned to see the soldier, Neanderthal, awash with light. Randall could feel his aches and pains vanishing as his body healed.

Both Neanderthal and Randall got to their feet with awed looks on their faces. Randall passed the rifle to Neanderthal, who raised its sight to his eye and spun on the spot, instantly switching into action mode.

Someone new had entered the fray; a man in a brown hooded cloak. He was approaching Tyrannogod and the eldritch beast with an easy loping stride.

Malcolm again emerged from the undergrowth and limped frantically towards the fight. He didn't move like a man, he moved like a deranged beast. The newcomer clicked his fingers and the professor became wrapped in ropes of golden light, completely immobilised.

"Who is that?" Neanderthal asked Randall.

"I don't know," Randall answered. "He didn't come with you?"

Neanderthal shook his head.

Tyrannogod stumbled, then fell. The dinosaur was gravely injured, his sides now covered in bleeding wounds and the imprints of the monster's suckers.

"Be gone from this place," the stranger commanded. His voice was quiet and calm, yet it carried an undertone of power.

The eldritch beast reared up again and squealed, sending its tentacles at the robed man. The stranger held his arms high and a glowing shield of raw energy emerged around him. The tentacles flopped uselessly against it, unable to break the barrier.

The stranger pointed an arm at Tyrannogod, who became wrapped in the same light that had healed Randall and Neanderthal moments ago.

The eldritch abomination shrieked in anger and attempted to charge the stranger. The robed man waved his hands through the air, and the trees at the edge of the clearing sprung to life. After a series of deep thudding groans, they advanced on the monster, walking on their slimy roots. The eldritch beast was enclosed in a tangled mess of branches.

It thrashed violently, ripping the trees to pieces as they formed a rudimentary prison around the monster. The forest had come to life and was on their side.

Screaming in frustration, the eldritch beast galloped from the clearing, carrying its horrendous stink with it. Its anguished wails quickly faded into the distance.

Tyrannogod got to his feet and nodded curtly at the cloaked stranger.

Neanderthal approached the man, with Randall following close behind. His face was completely obscured by his hood, revealing only the hint of a beard.

"Who are you?" the soldier asked.

"A man lost in the Dark World, as you are," he replied quietly. There was a flash and the man vanished.

Tyrannogod spoke up, causing Neanderthal to jump and point his rifle right at the dinosaur. "Lower your weapon, the threat is gone."

"A talking dinosaur..." Neanderthal mumbled, hesitantly lowering his gun.

Tyrannogod opened his jaws and gently brought them down on Malcolm Selleck, who was still bound by light. He lifted the mutated professor high and turned towards the village.

"Follow me," Randall said to Neanderthal.

"Where are we?" he asked.

"This is the Dark World. But don't worry, I'm working on a way out and you couldn't have arrived at a better time."

At last, Randall thought, he'd have some willing accomplices to get out of this place and back to Earth.

• • • • •

UPON THEIR RETURN to the village, they were greeted with a sea of relieved-looking faces. Neanderthal, shocked at the throng of bizarre monsters, was hesitant to follow Randall through the great wooden doors.

Tyrannogod walked off, still holding Malcolm, while Randall and Neanderthal were waved down by an enthusiastic William Carter.

The old man hobbled over, supported by a gnarled walking stick.

"Medical tent... over there!" he huffed. He pointed towards one of the large tepees that dotted the landscape.

"Oh, I think we are fine," Randall said quickly, but Carter ignored him.

He wondered if he looked as bad as the soldier did. While Neanderthal moved fine, he appeared as if he'd taken a beating.

"Expert on the Dark World now, are you? Get over there and you will be assessed!" Carter ordered.

Neanderthal gave Carter a curious look, then shrugged. His eyes darted back to the aliens by the far wall.

Randall and the soldier followed Carter along one of the flowing channels of energy towards the medical tent. They opened the flap and were greeted with a vast array of advanced medical equipment and machinery inside.

A series of green cylinders on the floor whirred and opened at the top, expelling a cloud of bugs. Only they weren't bugs, they were millions of nanomachines zooming straight towards Randall.

"Out!" Carter ordered, and Neanderthal was pushed outside by the old man's cane. The swarm engulfed Randall, blanketing his vision and choking his lungs. Then, it vanished.

"You're fine," Carter wheezed.

Randall stepped out of the tepee and swapped places with Neanderthal.

"Come in!" Carter called after twenty seconds.

Randall walked into the tepee and sat beside the smoking pool of yellow energy in the centre. Neanderthal looked the same, still heavily bruised with his eyes painted black and blue.

"Mobility looks good," Carter croaked as he surveyed the American soldier.

"Yeah, I'm feeling a lot less broken," Neanderthal grimaced. "In fact, I feel like I've been completely healed."

Randall waited to be addressed by one of the men.

"Randall Dare," Neanderthal smiled. "Your family, I tell ya… how you guys get wrapped up in this stuff I have no idea."

"When'd you meet my brothers?" Randall chuckled.

"Worked with Josh on a wendigo job. That's when I first met him. Then, I went to Heaven with him and after that to the magical land of Utgard. If I could get these places stamped in my passport, I'd look well-travelled."

"And now you're here."

"Yep, in the oddest place of them all. I still haven't quite processed the talking dinosaur."

Randall laughed again. Even Carter smiled at this.

Looking relieved to be getting off his feet, Carter gently shuffled into one of the nearby chairs.

"You said you've got a plan to get us out of here?" Neanderthal shot at Randall.

"I have ideas."

"How soon can you implement them?"

"Ahhh, I don't know... I don't really have a time frame. Maybe with Professor Selleck's help, all three of us can escape the Dark World."

"I assume he was the mutation being carried by Tyrannogod. He won't be leaving the Dark World," Carter interjected. "He is heavily corrupted by eldritch magic. It will be a miracle if we can bring him back to sanity at all."

Randall had somewhat expected this. The professor appeared to have lost his body and mind, yet he still wanted to hold out hope.

"What are all the creatures out there?" Neanderthal asked urgently, as if the question had been eating at him.

"Aliens, I guess," Randall shrugged.

"Werewolves, giants and now aliens. I don't think I'm getting out of this story alive. Lucky to have made it this far." Neanderthal shook his head.

"The human spirit perseveres, my good man," Carter beamed. Randall noticed the old man eyeing Neanderthal's military patches.

"Further to go yet," Randall began, but he was cut off again.

"That man who drove the monster away, who was he?" Neanderthal asked.

Carter looked at him with vague interest.

"A man appeared and helped us. Used healing magic on us and made the trees come to life. At least he looked like a man in a hooded cloak," Randall explained.

"We call him the traveller. Doesn't come to the village, instead lives up in a cave in the mountains," Carter answered.

"Does it matter?" Randall asked the US soldier sincerely.

"If I were a betting man, which I am, I'd bet my life savings that he was a god. He drove that monster away like it was nothing. If one of those abominations appears on Earth again, I'd like to know what he can teach us to deal with it."

"I guess we can go and ask him," Randall suggested. The stranger had seemed friendly enough during the monster attack, and the thought that he was a lost god from Earth had also occurred to Randall.

"That is a damn good idea," Neanderthal clapped his hands as he stood up.

"Oh, you want to go right now?" Randall said, taken aback.

"Yep."

"Is the journey safe?" Randall asked Carter.

"Yes. You can see the peaks of three mountains from the village. Climb the central mountain and you will find him," Carter yawned.

"What are they going to do with Malcolm?" Randall asked.

"The dinosaur isn't going to eat him, is it?" Neanderthal added, looking mildly concerned.

"There are some in the village with the knowledge to counteract eldritch magic. It is an imperfect system and the results are never guaranteed, but they will work to restore elements of the man within the monster."

"Right," Randall murmured. They would go and speak to the stranger in the mountain, then return and hope Malcolm had been cured.

"What are you thinking, Randy?" Neanderthal asked.

"Please don't call me Randy," Randall retorted.

"My bad, my bad," the soldier smiled, stripping his torn body armour off.

"I'll take that," Carter said. "We can fix it up for you."

Neanderthal passed his tattered gear to Carter before inspecting his rifle.

"Right now?" Randall affirmed.

"Unless it is wiser to wait for morning or daylight?" Neanderthal asked.

"There is no morning here, the light is always the same," Randall informed him.

Neanderthal didn't look particularly pleased by this revelation.

"The forest will be clear for some time. Everything will have fled the presence of the eldritch beast," Carter stated.

Neanderthal slung his rifle over his shoulder and nodded at Randall. "Let's go. You can fill me in on this place and what's happened to you on the way."

Randall, who'd spent the last ten minutes dumping adrenaline, didn't particularly feel like another adventure so soon after the last. Still, it felt like the right thing to do. The stranger who'd helped them had appeared human, though looks could be deceiving. Maybe he'd be another ally to help them escape. It was worth a shot.

Randall once again found himself facing the gloom of the forest as he and Neanderthal began the trek upwards into the mountains.

· · · · ·

CARTER HAD BEEN RIGHT. The forest was devoid of life as they climbed from the forest into barren fields of rock. Neanderthal likened hiking in the lower gravity to the time he'd flown through Heaven with winged shoes. Neanderthal began telling Randall his entire life story. The Navy SEAL had earned his nickname on a mission in Russia, where he'd used an ancient stone axe to take out a squad of enemy soldiers. His real name was Patrick Leeson, and he was a member of USSOT, currently leading a new team of specialists called Taskforce A. He'd had quite the career, having worked with Joshua Dare multiple times.

It seemed the story of Josh and Neanderthal's first encounter in the USA involved eldritch magic, though neither of them knew it at the time.

Randall was fascinated by the story of how the US soldier had ended up in the Dark World. He'd travelled with the same Australian team that had recruited Randall to a magical realm called Utgard, sometime after Randall's disappearance. Randall was pleased to hear that his brother Kane had been among them. That meant all three of the Dare children had been thrust into remarkable circumstances.

In Utgard, the team had been split into pairs and forced to enter a tournament. Neanderthal had no idea what'd happened to anyone else. Pair by pair, his group had disappeared through a dark archway to the whoops and roars of a crowd. Neanderthal had been teamed up with Malcolm Selleck to fight a flock of mythological harpies. Malcolm, teetering on the brink of obsession, had brought the Necronomicon into the stadium and unwittingly summoned the eldritch beast, which had wreaked havoc. Neanderthal had been gravely injured, then had suddenly arrived in the Dark World to see Tyrannogod approaching.

Once Neanderthal had finished talking, they began discussing the stranger who'd saved them earlier.

"It wasn't an alien," Neanderthal stated confidently. "I could see a human face beneath the hood, I'm sure of it."

"What about the magic he was using?" Randall questioned.

"He must be a god. That is the best explanation. If humans and dinosaurs can get lost in the Dark World, there is no reason to assume that gods can't be out here too."

Randall admitted that it was a sound theory. The god had the power to heal and command nature.

"Which gods have you met?" Randall asked him.

"First was Apollo. I met him in Japan. Then I met Hermes in Jerusalem. I helped rescue Hephaestus and Hecate from the Citadel of Heaven. Then, in another realm called the Dreamscape, I encountered Morpheus. Last was Artemis, who the AST recruited to their cause," Neanderthal counted aloud.

"All Greek then. I've only met Artemis," Randall replied, privately thinking that just encountering one god was more than enough. They seemed to be bad omens.

"You've met Sigurd, too," Neanderthal shrugged.

"He isn't a god, though."

"Even so, I think travelling with a mythological Norse warrior is something to be counted."

Randall laughed. This life was truly absurd.

He explained his proposed escape plan to Neanderthal, who

was immediately on board with every aspect of it. The soldier mainly wanted to know how many of the star spawn were awake in R'lyeh, a question Randall couldn't answer. He'd seen two, but had the impression that more of them were in the process of waking up.

They navigated steep portions of sharp black rocks as they clambered up the mountain. Randall was beginning to shiver, wishing he'd taken time to better prepare before the hike. They were being guided by an orange glow above them, shimmering out as a heavenly beacon in the dark. As they approached the source of the glow, a leering cave in a sheer cliff of black rock appeared.

The wind was roaring in a deafening gale, bringing with it the freezing cold. The glow of the fire inside the cave was extremely inviting.

"Hello?" Neanderthal yelled over the wind. "Anyone home?"

It was no good. Randall could barely hear Neanderthal and he was right next to him.

A shadow moved against the inner wall, growing in size as it approached. Then, a hooded figure appeared. He beckoned them forward.

Randall breathed a sigh of relief as the amazing warmth of the fire engulfed him. It seemed to flow into every corner of the cavern.

"Come now, it is freezing out there," the stranger murmured.

He moved two wooden stools in front of the fire before shuffling off into another chamber. Randall noticed he was wearing leather sandals.

The stranger quickly returned with two warm mugs of tea.

"Harvested from plants that grow here. It's bitter, but it'll do," he said apologetically.

"Works for me," Neanderthal said appreciatively.

Randall nodded enthusiastically in agreement.

The man lowered his hood, revealing shoulder-length brown hair, a long beard and striking blue eyes. He looked both unkempt and clean at the same time. He also looked jarringly familiar.

So familiar, in fact, Randall could've sworn he'd seen the face a million times.

It couldn't be who he thought it was.

"You've gotta be kidding me," Neanderthal spluttered, his tea rolling down his chin. His gaze was locked on the stranger's face, too.

Randall's eyes darted to the stranger's open palms. There were significant round scars in the middle of each.

"No," Randall stated in utter disbelief. Tyrannogod the Dinosaur King was one thing, but this? This couldn't be.

"Nice to meet you," the stranger smiled.

"You too," Randall stammered.

"Patrick Leeson, Navy SEAL. And this is Randall Dare," Neanderthal offered weakly.

"Judging by the looks on your faces I think you have guessed my name. But just for clarity, I am Jesus of Nazareth, and the pleasure is all mine."

CHAPTER 7

JESUS OF NAZARETH

"You are THE Jesus? Impossible," Neanderthal shook his head in utter disbelief.

Jesus gave the US soldier a knowing smile.

"But aren't you dead? What are you doing in the Dark World?" Randall asked.

"I know you will have a lot of questions, but drink the tea first. The cold of the Dark World isn't like the cold of Earth. It sits in your bones and gnaws away, if you allow it to," Jesus smiled.

The three of them sat in silence while Randall and Neanderthal slurped down the bitter contents of their cups. It made Randall feel a lot better.

"I didn't know you were real. Even though I went to Heaven and saw the angels I thought you might've just been a human or a prophet... what are you?" Neanderthal asked after draining his mug.

"For some reason, people don't like calling me this, even though it is the accurate term. I am a demi-god. My father was the Christian God and my mother was a mortal woman. And I was, for all intents and purposes, a prophet of my father's faith."

Randall chuckled. He'd never thought about it before, but it was true. Jesus was much the same as Hercules or any of the other half-gods from myth and legend.

"The most important prophet," Neanderthal added.

Jesus continued, "To answer your earlier question, I died and was resurrected. My father determined that my work on the Earth was complete, so I ascended to the City of Heaven, where I spent hundreds of years watching the world and watching my father."

"And just to clarify, your father was God, creator of the archangels?" Neanderthal asked.

"The very same."

Jesus stoked the fire further and it grew in intensity.

"Shouldn't you be like the archangels then? Impossibly powerful?"

"No. I am not like them. I am half-man, half-god. My power is limited. It is not tied to prayer and belief as theirs is; they were designed to be that way."

"You are the most famous person in history, you know?" Neanderthal said nonchalantly. "Your teachings have influenced countless generations across almost every country."

"I understand that it is difficult to separate my truth from legend. I watched the world for long enough to see my stories and teachings twisted to suit the purposes of individuals and organisations. I never intended to be this reverential figure, I just wanted to halt the corruption in my time. To teach people that there were better ways to be."

"To oversimplify," Neanderthal mumbled.

"Perhaps. Regardless of what my intentions were, I was but another pawn in my father's game. In the end, it seemed I played my role to perfection as all over the Earth I am honoured."

"You weren't on board with it all, then?" Randall asked. "Your crucifixion and the absolution of all of man's sins?"

A dark shadow crossed Jesus' face. He looked from Randall to Neanderthal, choosing his words carefully.

"I would never claim to have died the worst death. Many have suffered greater than I, yet those slow torturous days on that cross will forever haunt me. No sins were absolved. I died a martyr for my father and his quest for power. And I feel no shame to admit I was shaken for a long time. When I was resurrected, I was more than happy to be free of the Earth."

"Understandable," Randall shrugged.

"Yeah," Neanderthal agreed.

"Though you still haven't answered how you came to be here?" Randall asked again.

"What do you know of God on Earth?" Jesus asked the two men.

Neanderthal leaned back and pointed his feet towards the fire. "Well, we know that God hasn't been around for a long time. Archangel Michael leads the forces of Heaven with his six brothers. While their religions are still strong, the angels are seeking ways to cement their power so it doesn't fade."

Jesus nodded knowingly.

"Hence why we are on this mission to claim the power of Zeus," Neanderthal continued.

"Ah!" Jesus interrupted. "It all comes back to Zeus."

"What do you mean?" Neanderthal questioned.

"In the late eighth century, God was growing more agitated. At this point his power was phenomenal. What it would be today boggles the mind. He decreed that there would be no more prophets and set down far harsher rules for humanity than he had before. But I felt in my heart his anger wasn't truly about the behaviour of humans.

"He'd taken many solitary journeys to faraway lands, especially the ruins of Olympus. His attention was fixated on Zeus, who he'd known in long centuries past. I heard him whisper to himself as he studied ancient literature stolen in his wars. God was obsessed with finding out what happened to Zeus, the god-king who vanished. Though I was never able to confirm it, it was like a terror had gripped God. But what terror? He was unchallengeable.

"I made it my mission to understand what my father feared. I thought I could help in some way, but God was cagey. I confronted him, and God told me of his worry that his unnatural manipulation of the hierarchy of power had been noticed by things of greater stature than even he. He spoke of drums beating and flutes piping in the dark. He spoke of outer things teaching forbidden knowledge to humans. I didn't understand it. He was more powerful than any titan or primordial being.

"Not long after this, I began seeing *him*. A man in Heaven

I'd never seen before. He dressed like one of the great pharaohs of old. This Egyptian was no angel or god that I knew, yet he had a foreboding aura. He called himself a nameless messenger, and when he would appear, God would grow more erratic. In his paranoia, his dream of being Earth's only god disappeared. He feared the ancient and unknown fate of Zeus.

"Then, just like that, God vanished. He held counsel with his archangels, telling them Earth was now theirs to do with as they saw fit and fled to worlds unknown. I didn't understand it. Michael insisted I let it go, though even the mighty warrior that he is, he couldn't hide his concern. In secret, I made my return to Earth. Humans have an uncanny way of finding answers that couldn't be found in the endless libraries of Heaven or the rubble of Olympus. For a long, long time I had no luck until I met the Sundered King. Immediately he seemed untrustworthy, wielding eldritch magics that I had never seen before. He gave me a name, *Yog-Sothoth*, and sent me on a quest to summon him. I thought it was some god of the old world, long forgotten to history. As you know, I couldn't have been more wrong. I assembled the pieces to summon Yog-Sothoth and found myself pulled across worlds to the very boundaries of reality. Eyes and tentacles filled the skies as I was cast into this nightmare place. If I hadn't been a demi-god I would have surely died, well beyond the reaches of Heaven. Ever since, I have lingered here."

"Have you tried to leave?" Randall asked.

"For a long time, I sought a way to leave, but the answer to that problem always eluded me," Jesus sighed.

"Do you know the ruins of R'lyeh, somewhat near here in

the forest?"

Jesus nodded.

"The star spawn in the ruins have a device, a portal I think, that is aimed at Earth right now. When I was in there, I saw them test it and it failed. I think I know how to fix it, though it is a huge guess."

Randall explained his plan to reverse engineer the equation that got him here and input it into the star spawn's machine.

Jesus sat in thought for a long moment as he pondered this.

"This is a good plan," he said finally.

Neanderthal grinned triumphantly as if Jesus' approval automatically meant Randall was right.

"The main problem I see is that this portal device won't exclusively be star spawn technology. You cannot escape the Dark World without using its magic. I suspect that you will need the corruption of eldritch magic to use the device. All of the star spawn would be swimming in it."

Randall thought of the bubbling patch of eyes and tentacles on Tyrannogod, then of the corruption of Malcolm Selleck. He didn't want to end up like them.

"What are the long-term effects of this eldritch magic?" Neanderthal asked.

"It destroys you, eventually," Jesus answered. "The beings in the Village of the Lost have managed to stave off the corruption through the knowledge they've gained here. But if they ever were to leave, it would turn them mad."

"The knowledge they've gained here..." Randall thought. Something occurred to him.

"The nexus!" Randall exclaimed.

Neanderthal looked confused, while Jesus looked intrigued.

"Beneath the Village of the Lost is this kind of star of raw energy. I was told that if you touch it, Yog-Sothoth sees you and ends you. But I was also told that, if you were to survive, you'd be imbibed with the magic of the Dark World without the corruption."

Neanderthal still appeared painfully confused, but Jesus understood.

"There is no way to guarantee your safety at the moment Yog-Sothoth perceives you. Fate and luck would be your only guides," he said as he stroked his beard.

Again, Randall, the dis-believer, was contemplating destiny.

"Is there a way we can test if you can use the star spawn's tech before you do something reckless?" Neanderthal asked.

"I'd like to say yes... but the star spawn are waking up. The ruins could be crawling with them now. We may only have one shot to get in there and use the portal. Our success has to be guaranteed," Randall answered solemnly. He hated all the guesswork involved, but in his heart, he felt this was the case. After his last escape, he was sure the star spawn would've tightened security in the ruins.

"Why do you live alone in the mountains?" Neanderthal asked Jesus in an abrupt topic shift.

"I know that they are working on finding the weaknesses of the outer gods and I didn't want to draw Yog-Sothoth's attention to the village. I am a being of power beyond the usual residents of the Dark World and this can attract the wandering gaze of Yog-Sothoth."

Randall felt like Jesus was withholding information. Judging by the look on his face, Neanderthal thought so too.

"And?" the Navy SEAL prompted Jesus.

Jesus sighed. "The disappearance of Zeus has something to do with the outer gods. The flight of my father, God, is also directly tied to the outer gods. These were two of the most powerful and influential beings ever to walk the Earth and I am connected to them both. The residents of the village fear Yog-Sothoth, and rightly so, but I have always sought answers from the cosmic monster. From here I could freely wield my magic in attempts to commune with Yog-Sothoth in my quest to find answers. The fact I am still here after such a long time shows how successful I have been."

"Have you learned anything of value?" Randall asked.

"Well, yes. In learning how to grab the attention of Yog-Sothoth, I had to learn to break through the natural barriers that exist around him. For lack of a better way of saying it, I can annoy the outer god."

"Wait a second," Randall began, "does that mean you'd be able to use your magic effectively on a lesser being in the same order as an outer god?"

"What do you mean?" Jesus questioned.

"The great old one, Cthulhu, may have risen on Earth. In your prodding of Yog-Sothoth, you have gained knowledge no one else has. Knowledge that could help us fight Cthulhu! If you can get through the outer god's barriers, you can get through Cthulhu's magic," Randall deduced excitedly.

"I am not familiar with this being, but your logic may hold

true," Jesus affirmed hesitantly.

"In the ancient past, an alien race had to team up with Earth's primordial beings to subdue Cthulhu, and both of those are gone now. If he is awake again, you could be our only hope at countering him."

In Randall's mind, that settled it. Jesus had to return to Earth with them.

"How do you feel about returning to Earth?" Neanderthal asked Jesus. "Looks like the world may need you again."

"Still a lot of hunches and guesses..." Randall murmured.

"Do not forget, Randall, that here in the Dark World we are all influenced by Yog-Sothoth. All of your hunches and guesses could very well be the knowledge of Yog-Sothoth manifesting in your mind. As he is with us, we are with him," Jesus stated as he gazed into the fire.

"The less time spent with this alien overlord the better," Neanderthal grumbled, getting to his feet. "What do you say, Jesus? Will you come back with us to the village while Randall works on his equation?"

"Yes," Jesus answered. "Long have I wandered lost in the Dark World. It is time to step back into the light."

"There is potentially a war on the other side of this," Randall muttered.

"I am no stranger to violence and death. I will always pray for those who persecute me, but that does not mean I will shy away from doing what is right. To imagine me in war may seem silly with your legends and stories, but don't forget that as the sun rises on the good and evil equally, and the rain falls on the just

106

and unjust, that it also falls on me."

"Well, I'm motivated," Neanderthal said.

"Let's go," Jesus instructed.

"Maybe you can use your healing powers on Malcolm?" Randall suggested.

"The mutation from the forest? I will see what I can do, but his corruption runs deep..."

With that, the trio stepped back out into the wind. Though now, the warm glow of Jesus acted as a shield against the cold. Earth's greatest prophet was with them. For the first time since Randall had arrived, he was sure he was on the right track home.

CHAPTER 8

THE NEXUS

The days following their recruitment of Jesus flowed by in a tired blur as Randall desperately tried to understand the black hole equation that had brought him here. He sat in the library staring at the numbers and squiggles, willing them to make sense.

While Randall suffered among the towering tomes, Neanderthal travelled with Tyrannogod to the ruins by the crater on several scouting missions. He wanted intel on the numbers of the star spawn and the status of the teleporter Randall had used.

Jesus frequently vanished into the second medical tent where Doctor Selleck was being held by heavy restraints. Randall heard that he and War Snail were working long hours to ease the corruption in Malcolm's mind.

The air was heavy with apprehension as days passed. Each time Randall crossed the bridge over the flowing thought energy of Yog-Sothoth, he contemplated his untimely end. He imagined throwing himself into the river and seeing a million eyes turn on him. The time would soon come when he'd have to throw caution to the wind and do it.

The plan was simple. Once the equation was reverse-engineered, they'd head for the ruins right away. Randall guessed it'd been well over a week since the Australian team had arrived at the ruins of R'lyeh on Earth, and had potentially awoken Cthulhu. Every second they delayed their return was a second the Earth was at risk.

Randall found himself taking long walks around the internal perimeter of the village. He hoped the fresh air would spark an idea in him as he strolled in the shadow of the tall wooden wall. He still jumped every time a random shriek or cry echoed out from the nearby forest, often startling him out of his train of thought. Being a physicist, Randall understood that the physics he needed to understand was in the equation and not in the solution. The solution was just a bunch of numbers without context. Most equations sprang from simple postulates, like how the Schrodinger equation is essentially just a statement on energy conservation, or how all of general relativity came from the idea that light always moves at the same speed, no matter the reference frame.

One of the great questions he faced was how exactly the act of writing out an equation had brought him to the Dark World? He understood that equations enabled scientists to quantify and predict the behaviour of a physical system. Essentially, they were useful descriptions of reality. And yet, at the university, the mere action of writing out the Necronomicon's unsolved puzzle, and then solving it, had created a wormhole. He'd somehow interfaced with the very fabric of reality itself, as if the solution was analogous to a machine code executing a program on a computer. Where had the energy to open the portal come from? Was the Necronomicon acting as a conduit for some unknown power to alter reality? And if that was the case, why then did the star spawn need an advanced computer system to do the same? To create a stable wormhole, it was predicted that an advanced society would need to harness an unknown exotic matter with negative energy density. Of course, eldritch wizardry could also provide the answer to this, though that didn't really satisfy the scientist in Randall.

Randall suspected that his actions in New Zealand must've coincided with one of the star spawn's tests in the Dark World. The multi-dimensional machine in the ruins was currently pointed at Earth, and he knew it wasn't properly calibrated. If the device was advanced enough to problem solve its own errors, it could've recognised Randall's work in Dunedin as part of a solution to its problem, attempted to use the code, and thus generated a temporary wormhole. But it was the wrong code, going in the wrong direction. Instead of a stable wormhole to Sydney being opened up, the man at the code's source had been sucked in and dumped in the gloomy forest.

He wished he was back at his desk in Geneva working on a computational model. It would be a simple matter of running the code for various parameter regimes to identify the source of the machine's problem. He could play with locations and amounts of exotic matter until it worked. That was impossible here, with only books and paper at his disposal.

Rather unexpectedly, his long hours of staring at the Necronomicon equation eventually yielded positive results. He was in the library, drifting off after another long session, when a spark arrived like lightning in his brain. All of a sudden, it made sense!

Randall grabbed a lump of charcoal and a huge sheet of primitive paper and started scribbling. It was all there! The symbols and numbers moved together in a logical sequence. It had been in front of him the whole time. He'd been overthinking, trying to find complex solutions, when the answer was so simple. The solution to the equation was wave-like, meaning the equation itself had to have wave-like properties. It functioned through gravitational waves traversing dimensions!

Elated at his own brilliance, Randall wrote it out piece by piece. He knew how to make it work the other way. While it wasn't opening a portal here and now, he was sure that if he inputted into the portal device in the ruins, it'd get them home.

Randall rushed out of the library and towards the village centre, where he was met by Jesus.

"Ah Randall, I've been searching for you," the demi-god said.

"Jesus, I have good news," Randall started excitedly.

"As do I. Your colleague, Malcolm Selleck, has returned to sanity."

This shocked Randall.

"He desires to speak with you."

"Oh, umm, okay," Randall replied.

Jesus looked serene as ever in the dull light. The man always seemed to carry a godly aura of perfection with him as he moved. Though, there was a duality about him. His calloused carpenter's hands showed he existed as part of the real world too. Randall didn't really know how to take the guy.

"Right now?" Randall asked.

"Yes. The magic tying him back to his mind will not hold infinitely."

"Lead the way."

They traipsed across the village towards a tepee not too dissimilar from the medical tent they'd visited. One of the steaming channels of energy flowed into it, bathing it in a yellow glow. They were soon greeted by the booming footsteps of Tyrannogod, who followed them to the tent.

The front flap was closed as the trio approached, and Jesus asked Randall to wait while he checked on Malcolm.

Randall fidgeted nervously. He didn't want to be confronted with the professor's despair at his mutations. Maybe it was best if the man stayed as a mindless monster.

The flap lifted and Jesus beckoned Randall in.

There were two others inside, War Snail operating a host of impressive machinery and William Carter leaning on his cane. Tyrannogod poked his enormous head through the flap to join the conversation.

Lying on a raised bed was the monstrous visage of Malcolm Selleck, with his purple skin and engorged eyeball. His long tentacle arm was still bound with thick leather belts to the bed's railing.

"Randall," Malcolm smiled. He looked tired, like the weight of the world was on his shoulders.

"Doctor Selleck," Randall nodded politely. "It is good to see you."

"I am glad that I cannot see me," Malcolm laughed as he looked down at his tentacle arm.

"It is a... unique look," Randall murmured, feeling stupid.

"This is what happens when you meddle in the unknown. The risks of scientific curiosity can be greater than we are often led to believe," Malcolm stated.

"How did they get you back?" Randall asked. When he'd seen Malcolm in the forest, all traces of humanity had been lost.

"I can answer that," the haggard old voice of Carter chimed in. "You know the artefact that powers this village?"

"The Stone of Ebiziad," Randall answered.

"Yes, yes. Great power in that rock. Proximity to it calmed Malcolm and eased the corruption in his mind."

"Excellent," Randall said happily. "Just let him carry the rock around then."

"Can't be done," War Snail said.

"Yes, quite right, Snail. The Stone of Ebiziad flows with a raw power we don't understand. Overexposure results in death," Carter added.

"Oh," Randall said lamely.

"There aren't often easy answers. But that is why we are scientists," Malcolm sighed.

"I have a plan to get us out of here, Doctor Selleck," Randall offered an encouraging smile. "We will take you with us."

Malcolm chuckled weakly, "Look at me. I am mutated and deformed beyond recognition. Apparently, I need to be in close proximity to a magical stone just to regain my mind. You're a smart kid, Randall, smart enough to know that I'm not leaving this place."

Randall saw War Snail give a solemn nod in the background. Carter hobbled forward and rolled up his left sleeve. Randall recoiled when he saw the old man's skin.

"Why do you think I am still here? I too am cursed by Yog-Sothoth. I traded my ability to return home for unnatural life. I feared death…"

Carter's arm wasn't quite as purple as Malcolm's tentacle, but it was an unnerving shade of violet. Suckers ringed with small hooks ran its length up and down.

"The one thing we all have here is time," Carter continued.

"And in time we will find a way to undo what was done to us," Tyrannogod added, his head still poking through the tent flaps.

"I have a family, Randall. Two girls and a wife. Tell them that I love them and that I wish I could be there for them. Tell them I'm always watching over them," Malcolm said with some urgency.

"I will. Of course, I will," Randall nodded.

"And I'm sure you already understand this, but the Necronomicon can no longer be used. It is a tool designed for temptation and madness."

Randall decided it was best not to tell him about the fully translated version of the black book just below them in the library.

"If Neanderthal, Jesus and I make it back to Earth we will ensure that no one uses the book again," Randall affirmed.

"How are you making it back to Earth?" Malcolm asked.

"The star spawn in the ruins near here have a portal. It wasn't operational the last time I was there, and I think I know why. I have reverse-engineered the equation that sucked me into the Dark World. I think, if I can input a new sequence into the device, it will take us home. It's just a theory though."

"A good theory," Malcolm smiled.

"Yeah, I just need the blessing of Yog-Sothoth and I can try it." Randall had taken to the idea of calling eldritch magic without the corruption 'Yog-Sothoth's blessing' ironically.

Malcolm looked alarmed.

"In theory, it is not like the curses we are afflicted with," War Snail interjected, seeing the professor's look of shock. "His 'blessing of Yog-Sothoth' will allow him to interact with all the bio-machinery around here. It will not physically alter Randall, though it may scramble his mind a little."

"Well… who am I to argue with the legendary William Carter, a robotic snail and a dinosaur," Malcolm yawned. He was fading fast.

"You'd all best leave him be," War Snail commanded.

"Yes, come now Randall Dare. If you have successfully reverse-engineered your equation, that means it is time to step into the mind of the oldest monster in creation," Tyrannogod stated.

Randall shook Malcolm's hand vigorously and repeated his promise to find the man's family. Giving the mutated professor one last look, Randall left the tent. Tyrannogod had lowered himself to the ground.

"I thought giving people rides embarrassed you," Randall smirked.

"With what you are about to undertake, I feel your needs outweigh mine," the dinosaur replied seriously.

Randall mounted Tyrannogod and they marched towards the library. War Snail departed Malcolm's tent and followed them, while Jesus went to fetch Neanderthal.

"This is all happening a bit quickly," Randall thought. He'd only just solved the equation, and he was already on the way to the nexus.

They descended the stairs by the black cube and crossed the mesmerizing river of energy. Tyrannogod calmly walked through the library Randall had become so familiar with. Again, they came before the shining orb of raw power floating in mid-air.

The group stood in silence as Randall hopped off Tyrannogod and stepped ahead of the others.

"Good luck," Neanderthal said, clapping him on the back. The soldier was wearing his full military kit, complete with newly repaired body armour.

Jesus didn't speak, he just looked at the orb curiously.

"Are you sure this is how you want to proceed?" War Snail asked Randall.

"I can't explain it, but it feels like the right thing to do..." Randall said hesitantly. He wasn't lying. The pulsating orb of energy was transfixing. Its rhythmic flashes of colour called to him in a primal way. He had to touch it.

"Once more into the abyss," Randall said quietly.

Resolute, Randall walked until he was directly under the star. He was just tall enough that if he stood on his tippy-toes he could touch its surface.

Randall breathed in deeply and stretched his arm high above his head.

His fingers brushed the cold fire of the orb. Everything went black.

CHAPTER 9

YOG-SOTHOTH

He blinked. Randall's blurry surroundings came into focus. He knew this place...

This was Cairns! He was in his childhood home in Australia.

But how could that be? Surely it wasn't real... It had to be an illusion generated by the nexus. Yet, the pictures of family on the oddly coloured walls seemed so tangible. He could smell the freshly mown grass outside. He could see the distant trees by the top of the driveway swaying in the breeze. He was home.

Randall heard a strangled yowl at his feet. His family's old grey cat, creatively named Maow, had hobbled up and was nuzzling his feet.

But wait... that wasn't right. Maow was dead. He'd died a couple of years ago.

"This reality has been generated from my memories," Randall thought,

scratching the old cat on the head.

"Quite right," a familiar voice said.

Randall turned quickly.

A familiar figure was wandering down the hallway from his old bedroom. It was... it was him, only a couple of years younger.

"Yog-Sothoth?" Randall asked cautiously.

"I suppose," the doppelganger said, picking up a small statuette on the kitchen countertop and observing it closely.

"Well, I guess what I can comprehend of Yog-Sothoth," Randall shrugged, thinking back to his discussion with William Carter.

"And what I can comprehend of you, Randall Dare."

"Why are we here, in this memory of my home?" Randall asked.

"I suspect your mind has taken you to a place of comfort, rather than dealing with the reality of your situation."

"And what is my situation."

Randall's copy clicked his fingers.

The world went dark. Randall felt his skin stretching. His eyes were being torn from his skull. He could feel suckers ringed with needles piercing his skin. His limbs were being stretched in all directions. It was pain beyond imagining. He began to scream, but the vision faded as quickly as it had arrived.

The pain was gone. They were back in the memory.

"Are you going to kill me?" Randall asked.

"I shouldn't think so."

"What are you, exactly?"

"As you guessed, I am a manifestation of Yog-Sothoth,

viewed through the lens of you. What little you can perceive of me has been processed in your mind and presented suitably for your understanding."

Randall immediately saw a problem with this.

"So," Randall started, "this conversation is being heavily influenced by my unconscious mind, then?"

"Do you think a being such as Yog-Sothoth, whose body manifests as an entire dimension external to the physical universe, has casual conversations?"

"Well, I don't know... maybe," Randall shrugged. He had, after all, met the Goddess Artemis. She looked and spoke like an ordinary person.

The fake Randall laughed as he sat down on the living room couch. "Such a comparison is not accurate."

Randall didn't really care. He was here for one thing only; he had to be infused with eldritch magic.

"How long will it take? For my goal to be completed, I mean," Randall asked.

"A moment and an age," Yog-Sothoth muttered.

"Will I become a monster, like Malcolm Selleck?"

"No."

"Well, that's a plus at least," Randall thought.

Randall stood in awkward silence for a minute, wondering if he should try to make small talk with this all-powerful being. Though he wasn't really speaking with Yog-Sothoth, he was speaking with a fragment of the creature through the lens of his own perception. But this could be a plus, Randall thought. It meant if he asked questions, he may be able to get answers shaped in a way that he could understand.

"What are you, exactly?" Randall asked at last.

"In your world, I am classed as an outer god. Though I am much more than this. Yog-Sothoth is second only to Azathot. My existence threatens creation, so I linger out here, on the fringe. I long to be in the universe, like the early days..."

"And who is Azathot?" Randall asked.

The fake Randall scratched his chin and looked to the roof.

"He is known as Chaos. Reality is but his dream. In your eyes, he would appear as a great storm in the centre of everything. The black clouds pulse with red lightning, and your ears are assaulted with the banging of drums and the piping of flutes. These sounds, while deafening to you, keep Azathot asleep. For if he were ever to wake, everything would end in that instant."

Randall gulped. That didn't sound good. But perhaps this was just the religion of this creature. Much in the same way Christians believed God was the be all and end all of reality, so Yog-Sothoth believed this to be the case with Azathot. Randall found it strange that in all his discussions about outer gods since arriving here, he hadn't once heard the name Azathot.

The fake Randall, reading his thoughts, immediately replied, "Religions worship gods. But above gods are titans, and above titans are primordials, and above primordials is Azathot. He birthed them all, millions of them, all across the universe. This is no story; this is the truth of your reality."

"Did he dream them all into existence?" Randall asked.

"No, in the beginning, he was awake. There was a cataclysm... a great cataclysm. Beyond what even I can understand. Azathot is the reason that creatures like gods break the physical laws of the universe, the ones you study. If it weren't for him, there would be no magic, no divinity..."

This piqued Randall's interest. He'd just accepted, in the short time that he'd been aware of it, that the supernatural was just some unexplainable part of the world, completely removed from the rules that governed reality. Perhaps it was understandable after all.

"Explain this great secret to me," Randall demanded.

"It is no secret, there are just none who know. You understand the Kardashev scale, I assume?"

Of course Randall understood the Kardashev scale. It was developed by Nikolai Kardashev in 1964 and measured a civilisation's technological advancement by the amount of energy it harnessed. It usually featured three levels. A type one civilisation could harness all the energy available on its planet. Type two meant harnessing a star through means such as a Dyson sphere, and type three meant being able to utilise the power of a galaxy. Some scientists had even added two more tiers to describe civilisations with the power of a universe behind them. Current humanity hadn't even reached type one status yet.

"Extend the scale to type five and you can begin to understand Azathot's origins. Imagine a civilisation with total mastery of every aspect of reality. Before your universe was born there was another plane of creation. In this reality, foreign even to the comprehension of higher beings, was a civilisation that reached the pinnacle of its power. There was an event, the details of which none but Azathot know. Something terrible happened, an experiment of unimaginable consequence, and reality collapsed around the being Azathot. He was at the epicentre of this great destruction. The power that ended that reality exploded your universe into being. The big bang... a fresh universe. And into this new space fell Azathot, broken and charred, a being that survived from another form of creation. He did not exist within the laws of your new universe. Desperate to preserve what was lost, Azathot used his powers. I, Yog-Sothoth, was born first. I was designed to be a partner, to help Azathot rebuild in his loss and despair. But he soon learned that he could not bring back what was gone forever... He came to embrace the idea of the new universe, which he existed inside but was not a true part of. I, on the other hand, was part of the universe as I was built in it. Azathot saw my influence spread as worlds fell into my grasp... becoming parts of me."

Randall shuddered at the thought of entire planets of countless eyes and writhing tentacles reaching far into their horizons.

"And so, I was cast out. But in time other outer gods were born, then the great old ones. Nyarlathotep, in his glee and malevolence, gave natural life the power to reach me, to call to me in my exile. And I reached out to them. He plays games, Nyarlathotep... games that can't be won...

"And so Azathot birthed a kind of being different from the outer gods. From him spewed the primordials, beings representing tangible concepts in the physical universe. They helped form worlds and create life, yet they were still children of Azathot. They were born of a being beyond creation, and so the rules of reality didn't apply to them. This immunity to the universe was passed into their children, the lesser beings of titans and gods, who can fly through the air and create something out of nothing. They can control, twist and transform at their will, all because of Chaos, who is to them unknowable and unexplainable. But even they understand, through the myths of their own kind, and deep within their psyches, not to seek Azathot; the storm in the centre of all things."

"In case they wake him up," Randall added.

"Yes, though this is wrong," Yog-Sothoth yawned. "Azathot cannot be woken until the end of the universe. Nothing can, except me... Only I, who mirrors the creator in power, can end the beating of drums in the dark."

Randall thought he saw a malevolent gleam glimmer through his doppelganger's eyes. It was clear that Azathot had damn good reasons for banishing Yog-Sothoth.

"Is there a way to kill an outer god?" Randall asked. There was no point trying to hide his thoughts, as this thing could read them all anyway.

"All things that are born can die," the fake Randall said, giving him a curious look.

"How?"

"I could not explain it to you because your kind is so far from being at that level. To be able to challenge a being like Nyarlathotep, your species would have to have mastery of both your universe and an ally of infinite divine power. You would have to be on the same level of civilisation that Azathot was when he destroyed his own universe. Every dimension your playground, with every atom bending to your whim…"

"Right. That means Nyarlathotep is a potential problem that we can't get rid of. What about Cthulhu? I've been told that the primordials shut him down once. How can we do it in a world with no primordials?" Randall asked.

"Cthulhu can be physically overpowered. That is why he has an army. He is extraordinarily powerful, far beyond the standard gods of your world, but he is by no means invincible."

"I need more," Randall demanded. He didn't want time to run out without a way to defeat this problem back on Earth.

"The alien race that built those cities of black stone on your world, the elder things, they fought with Cthulhu on and off for thousands of years, often finding victory. You must remember that Cthulhu is a higher being, and as such is susceptible to things you don't understand. He feels the movements of the stars galaxies away. Cosmic events in the far-off universe can render him crippled. That is how they beat him the first time. The primordials waited for a moment in cosmic time when the alignment of certain worlds would leave Cthulhu weakened, then with the elder things they moved on his heartland of R'lyeh, striking the city and sealing Cthulhu away for a long, long time."

"That's all well and good, but we don't have alien armies or knowledge of far-off cosmic alignments to use. And even if we did, we don't have thousands of years to wait around," Randall cautiously replied. He wanted an easier answer.

"If you are looking for a simple solution to a complex problem you will not find it. You are on the right track though. The being you have allied yourself with, Jesus of Nazareth, for all his compassion and virtue, is a weapon against Cthulhu."

"Jesus isn't a warrior. He is a healer and philosopher."

"He is gifted. He learned to break through my barriers and he is linked to an incredibly powerful being. His father, God, hides away in a dark corner of the distant universe with his immense power, afraid... yet, God remains a mighty well that Jesus of Nazareth can draw from, if he learns how."

"Afraid of what?" Randall asked.

"Me," the doppelganger smiled.

Randall was unnerved to see such a sinister look cross his own face.

"God can't help us, I don't think..." Randall muttered.

"No, but Jesus is part of an order of immensely powerful creatures worshipped on the Earth. God left his mark on your world in the form of raw power. Combine the abilities of the new gods, the archangels, with the old gods and see victory become possible. Jesus is your link to the forces of God. Should his knowledge from the Dark World be allied with the power found on your planet, I can see Cthulhu being toppled."

"As simple as that?" Randall asked.

"Perhaps... though Nyarlathotep once again walks on your world. He seeks to find God and punish him... This could be a problem to your quest."

"Why do you outer gods care about God anyway? Isn't he just some upstart from a small planet?" Randall asked. The scale of the outer gods was so enormous he didn't understand why they would care about puny Earth deities.

"There are rules the gods must follow and customs they

should abide by. Do you remember, just now, that I told you the primordials represented physical aspects of the universe? They are a blend of this reality and the extra-universal being Azathot, and as such, have the power within them to irreparably damage the universe. Usually, gods can only act within their own domains, so their power is limited. Yet, we placed rules on the primordials in the early days, to be passed down their generations, to not risk damaging the universe. Remember, the power inside every divine being comes from Azathot, a creature not of this creation, and as such it doesn't belong. That power could destroy everything. Admittedly, for the kind of destruction I'm talking about, the abuse would have to be mind-bogglingly large and widespread. That is why we made the rules."

"What are these rules that the gods have to follow?"

"Life is one example. It is sacred above all things as it is powered by souls; whether large or small, simple or complex. Some divine beings are born with life and death in their domains, and as such are trusted to wield that power responsibly. Unfortunately, it seems most gods and titans have the innate ability to manipulate life. Souls are powerful pockets of energy, you see, and if that power is not respected, small actions can lead to great consequences. That is why gods are forbidden from manipulating life and death unless it is their birthright to do so."

"So, you outer gods act like police, then?"

"Nyarlathotep does... but he likes games. He walks across space and time, planning things and taking perverse joy in slowly punishing those who break our laws."

"Right, that means God broke one of your laws, then? That's

why he fled from the world?" Randall said, putting it all together.

"What God did was an affront and a perversion of the divine order, but he didn't strictly break any laws. He saw how divine energy magnified in strength as it flowed upwards, and he manipulated it. He created beings to channel that power and further increase its ferocity. He then set about removing the other gods from your world so he could have unnumbered worshippers. The power he holds now is phenomenal, with you little humans in your billions believing in him. He was clever and inventive, a true outlier among the gods. But he saw what became of the God-King Zeus and grew scared. Scared of us and of Azathot, when he learned the truth of creation. Nyarlathotep had been watching him for some time, and when God learned what he truly was, he ran."

"This is all very interesting," Randall said. He picked Maow up and placed the old grey cat on his lap. If he understood the core of the conversation correctly, Jesus had the potential to weaken Cthulhu enough for him to be taken down by the divine forces of Earth.

"I think I've learned everything I need to from you," Randall said, absent-mindedly stroking the purring cat. "Just one more question; why would you care if gods broke rules and damaged the universe?"

"Well, I don't," Yog-Sothoth shrugged. "I would survive the ending of all things. Nyarlathotep, as he can wander the universe freely, prefers to keep an eye on all we have discussed. He may also be an outer god, but he is not like me. None match Yog-Sothoth, as I am infinite. If I ever can return in full to the universe, I will tear it apart, and much like my father before me, build a new reality in my image."

"Well, I sincerely hope that you never make it into the universe," Randall said curtly.

"A hope shared by all you brief flickers of mortal life," the fake Randall laughed.

"Can I go now? Or will I be destroyed like all others who have touched the nexus?"

The fake Randall observed him with a relentless piercing gaze. "You, Randall Dare, will be the ant that escapes the scorching blaze of the magnifying glass. Good luck with your flight from the Dark World. You will need it in the days to come."

Randall felt a sudden electric shock travel from his core to his extremities. He felt the ground beneath him and smelled the stale air. He was back in the library!

"Are you alright?" the calming voice of Jesus sounded in his ears.

Randall groggily opened his eyes and got to his feet. He'd been lying spread-eagled in the dirt.

"Yeah, I think so," he said, checking himself up and down.

"What did you see?" Tyrannogod asked.

"A memory... but Yog-Sothoth was in it. Only, he was me, but from the past..."

"Fascinating," War Snail murmured. "Why'd he let you go?"

"I don't know. He told me the nature of gods and the universe and everything, then just released me. I guess I asked the right questions."

"Right!" Neanderthal interjected, clapping Randall on the

back. "You got out alive, that's all we needed. Are you ready to assault the ruins of R'lyeh?"

"Yes," Randall answered.

"Then let's get this show on the road!"

Randall looked across the motley group he'd assembled.

"We will help you breach the ruins," Tyrannogod affirmed.

"Then you are on your own," War Snail added.

The dinosaur and snail had been good friends to Randall during his time here, though he hadn't appreciated them more than right now.

Randall turned to Jesus. "It seems a lot is on your shoulders, Jesus. I know you were already used as a tool by the divine, but it may have to happen again. The magic you have learned here, in combination with other divine powers on Earth, seems to be the key to beating Cthulhu."

Jesus frowned as he contemplated this.

Eventually, he spoke, "I have always suspected this would be the case. Many versions of my religion have written of my second coming when I announce myself again at the end of all things. But perhaps I am not the herald of this disaster, instead, Cthulhu is, and I will make myself known to the world again to stop him."

"It sounds like you will have to fight," Neanderthal surmised.

"The world is my home, not Heaven or any other realm. I would not see it fall into the hands of a monster willingly."

"Good to hear," Neanderthal stated.

Feeling determined, Randall led the group out of the library. He felt sure the plan was going to work. They were going home.

CHAPTER 10

RETURN TO EARTH

Neanderthal insisted the group get a few hours of sleep before they journeyed to the ruins. Randall tossed and turned, his mind ablaze with excitement and apprehension. His short time in the Dark World had revealed a side of himself he'd never known. Gone was the timid teenager who avoided confrontation and lived with a ceaseless, perpetual existential dread. Sure, he self-admitted, he'd mustered the courage to move to Geneva. But even so, deep down inside he'd imagined that would be the most adventurous thing he'd ever do.

'Now look at me. I've escaped ruins full of monsters. I charged into a battle between a dinosaur and an eldritch monster and even willingly stepped into a nexus of energy, despite knowing it could kill me,' Randall smiled. He was a man reborn in the dim light of the squashed ovals above. And now his greatest test waited; the storming of the ruins.

The plan was for stealth and subterfuge, only fighting if they met resistance in the portal room. Neanderthal was well equipped and Jesus had magic on his side. They'd hold off the star spawn while Randall navigated the computer system. Now that Randall was infused with eldritch magic, he hoped the system would respond to his thoughts alone. That was best case scenario. The worst was being stranded in that room with no way out, but he didn't want to think about that potential outcome.

It was stuffy in Randall's tepee. The air was thick with moisture and the humidity was growing unbearable. There was no way he was going to sleep, so Randall decided to get up. It was a good idea to re-draw the equation out in the dirt, just to be ultimately sure he remembered it.

Randall opened the flap and felt a cool breeze tickle his skin. The village was quiet, the still buildings bathed in the yellow glow of the energy channels crisscrossing the ground. Randall looked towards the top of the wooden perimeter wall and noticed something peculiar. The wailers, bound by their heavy chains, were acting oddly. They appeared agitated as they writhed and struggled against their binds.

Then Randall noticed the breeze carried a familiar stink on it. He'd last smelled it in the ruins of R'lyeh...

Something was wrong. The wailers began screaming at the top of their lungs.

BOOM!

The wooden wall was blown apart in an earth-shattering explosion.

Randall ducked for cover as splinters of wood rained down

from the sky.

BOOM!

The main gate vanished in a cloud of smoke and wood. The guard wailers shrieked as they were thrown through the air into the village.

Randall peered through the smoke as it swiftly cleared. Something was moving among the gloomy trees of the forest. It looked like a turret, pointing right at the hole in the wall.

Randall felt a body slam into him and pull him down, right as a glowing projectile zoomed overhead and collided with colossal force against Tyrannogod's cavern.

The rocks tumbled over one another, partially blocking the entrance.

Randall was pulled to his feet by the back of his jacket.

"Let's go!" Neanderthal shouted, sprinting away. Randall followed as best he could, though, despite his lack of equipment, he was still slower than the soldier.

A series of explosions echoed through the village as projectiles rained down from the sky. Every creature that called the place home was now awake and scrambling in the face of the attack, attaching their clumsy armour and reaching for weapons.

Randall, caught in a cloud of debris, smashed right into the side of a large brown object. It was War Snail's shell!

The cyborg insect's mechanical eyestalks were waving frantically back and forth.

"What's going on?" Randall puffed.

"The star spawn are here," War Snail answered as he pointed both hands towards the darkness of the forest. With a spark, his missile-like fingers detached and shot into the tree line. They exploded with deafening force, generating tall mushroom clouds of flame. The village glowed orange in the aftermath of the explosion. Bathed in the light of the forest fire, Randall could, at last, see what was out there.

The star spawn, in their legions, were advancing through the trees. Their cephalopod heads with long tentacles cast dreadful shadows as they marched. They were all heavily armoured and appeared to be carrying weapons. On both sides of their right wrists sat long tubular objects pulsing with green light. One of the star spawn pointed its tubes towards them and fired a series of super-heated plasma blasts. Again, Randall found himself face to face with the dirt as he dived for cover.

War Snail felt the brunt of the attack, squealing as his skin sizzled.

"Are you okay?" Randall yelled over the noise.

War Snail made an electric gargling sound and lifted his head. The outer sides of his shell detached and sprang forward on mechanical prongs, forming a shield in front of him. Then, two formidable Gatling guns unpacked themselves and mounted on the shield. They spun to life and fired a hail of bullets at the approaching army.

This drew another hail of plasma fire from the trees.

Randall wasn't staying here. He commando crawled away from War Snail towards a large rock that had been blown from Tyrannogod's home. Crouching behind it like a scared little boy, Randall assessed his situation. Things had grown wildly out of control in minutes. Flashes from advanced weaponry lit the entire place up in a multi-coloured glow as explosions shook the ground.

The forest was on fire. The flames revealed more than just the star spawn. There was machinery as well, more biotech like he'd seen in the ruins. Large hovering tanks with long turrets pushed through the undergrowth towards the village. They shot projectiles that ripped their targets asunder.

But why were the star spawn attacking here?

Randall peered around the rock and saw a human holding a rifle advancing at the head of a host of aliens. It was Neanderthal, and he was in full soldier mode. The American appeared to be leading a hastily established defence force against the aliens. His rifle fire cut clearly through the noise of the attack.

One of the star spawn ran at Neanderthal on all fours like a charging silverback gorilla. Neanderthal fired, but his shots did nothing against the monster's bio-armour. The monster lunged and Neanderthal dropped to the ground. The star spawn warrior landed on top of him, its legs on either side of the soldier's body. It ripped at his body armour, tearing chunks of it away. Neanderthal released his rifle and drew his pistol, firing two clean shots up into the monster's tentacles. The bullets found their mark on a soft spot, and the star spawn fell dead.

Randall ran towards the soldier, and with great difficulty, pulled the hulking green body off Neanderthal.

"Thanks," Neanderthal muttered, picking up his rifle and pointing it towards another attacker. Several waves of plasma bullets rocketed towards them, causing Randall to uselessly hold his arms over his face. They were saved by one of the residents of the village, an alien made of gas, expanding around them and absorbing the blasts.

The American began barking orders at his allies as the nearest wave of the star spawn pushed into the village.

A reptilian alien that Randall had encountered several times slinked up a portion of the perimeter wall and waited for a star spawn to pass. Randall saw dripping fangs emerge from the alien's mouth as it dived on its prey, biting it and causing the star spawn to instantly start convulsing.

The reptilian slithered toward another victim but was caught in a hail of plasma. It flopped dead, covered in horrific burns. Randall gulped. He didn't want to end up like that poor creature.

Neanderthal plucked a grenade from his belt and tossed it at the star spawn horde. It exploded in a shower of shrapnel, scattering the octo-men from their military lines.

"Randall, listen to me," Neanderthal said, sending more rounds flying into the darkness. "Find Jesus. If the star spawn are here, now is our best chance to get in the ruins!"

Randall nodded.

ROARRRRRR!

The ground shook as a large rock was pushed away from the village's central mound. Tyrannogod emerged, looking dirty and furious. The dinosaur stampeded into the fray, leaping right onto one of the enemy tanks, which smashed into the dirt with a squelching groan. Tyrannogod gripped its turret in his jaws and snapped it off. Like a dazzling light show, plasma bolts shot at the dinosaur from all directions, but the hulking T-Rex was already moving. He scooped up a star spawn in his jaws and crunched, ripping the octo-man to pieces. Tyrannogod shook his head and thundered to the other side of the village, stepping on every tentacled foe in his path.

Randall ducked beneath a tank blast and jumped over one of the yellow energy channels. Just to the right he could see a shining orb. It had to be Jesus using his magic.

Click, click, click.

One of the star spawn was moving towards Randall, its beady black eyes focused right on him. It raised its right arm and fired. Two super-heated jets of plasma careened through the air towards him. Randall squeaked, helpless.

The air became thick with smoke and Randall lost sight of the star spawn and its plasma bolts. His ears filled with a buzzing sound and he realised it wasn't smoke! He was shielded by nanomachines!

The swarm dissipated once the plasma bolts had been absorbed. The star spawn tilted its head curiously, its tentacles waving wildly. It aimed again.

There was a crash as one of the bio-tanks slammed into the attacking star spawn. With a hiss of steam, its entry hatch opened and a withered figure scrambled out.

"Randall, my boy," Carter croaked. "Help me down, will you?"

Randall rushed to the side of the hover tank and gently helped lower William Carter to the ground.

The tank was a sickly grey colour and looked like it was comprised of thick layers of veins, with the upper portion and turret being gleaming metal. Just touching the tank to help Carter left Randall coated in slime.

"How the hell did you end up inside an enemy tank?" Randall asked, utterly flabbergasted.

Carter picked up his cane and wiped the sweat and slime from his forehead. "All a bit of a blur, actually."

"You can drive it?" Randall questioned.

"I believe this device can't distinguish between one of these wretched star spawn and the corruption of Yog-Sothoth," the old man said very enthusiastically.

This was perfect. If Randall got in the tank, he could test if he had successfully been imbibed with eldritch magic by trying to drive it.

A nearby explosion knocked both Randall and Carter off their feet.

"Carter, can you guard this tank for me?" Randall asked as he got back up. He gently helped the old man to his feet, somewhat impressed the old man could take such a fall in his stride.

Carter raised his eyebrows incredulously. What Randall had just asked was ridiculous.

"Actually, find shelter. I'm sure the tank will be fine."

"Find your allies and get out of this place," Carter said. "If this is happening here, the attack may have commenced on Earth. Save our world, Randall Dare."

"I'm going to," Randall replied, resolute. "Can the village win this fight?"

"Don't forget that the beings here have come from infinite worlds and times and that we have objects of tremendous power," Carter winked.

Randall dashed away from Carter towards the shining light again.

Jesus was just ahead. He had his arms raised high, generating a shield around a large group of residents of the Village of the Lost. They had weapons of their own and were taking the fight to the star spawn, protected by Jesus' magic.

Randall rushed through the shield and came to the side of Jesus.

"We need to get Neanderthal and go!" Randall sputtered.

"I, too, had this thought. Where is he?" Jesus asked.

"There!" Randall said, pointing downhill towards a clearing full of battling warriors. In the middle of them was Neanderthal.

Randall watched as the US soldier ran straight into the path of a bio-tank, plucked a grenade from his belt, jumped and threw it down the turret. The tank exploded into a cascade of fleshy pieces.

"He is quite capable," Jesus admitted. "How do you intend on getting out of the village. Through the forest?"

"There is a tank just up the hill. The three of us can get in it and drive it out of here. I doubt the star spawn will fire on their own."

Jesus raised his left hand and pointed it at Neanderthal. With a sucking of air, the Navy SEAL was hoisted from his feet and drawn towards them at phenomenal speed. Looking dazed, he focused on Randall and Jesus.

"Can we abandon the beings of the village?" Randall asked Jesus.

"I have blessed each and every one of the creatures here who fight against the dreaded star spawn. Though I will be away from this fight, I will be with them."

That was good enough for Randall. As much as he felt for the plight of the aliens, his home world was calling him.

Tyrannogod's primal roar diminished all other sounds as he stood on a pair of star spawn. They were climbing the dinosaur like cockroaches on a kitchen bench. The T-Rex ripped one of the star spawn from his back with his jaws and sent several others flying with a powerful tail sweep, where they met the powerful Gatling guns of War Snail. The cyborg was still in this fight and shredding the star spawn in hails of bullets.

The residents of the village certainly weren't going down without a fight. Randall saw the cloud of nanomachines rising up, protecting aliens all across the battlefield, though it seemed to thin and diminish each time it took the brunt of waves of plasma fire.

All of the tepees were now either on fire or torn to shreds. The stone buildings and mud huts had been obliterated in the onslaught. It was chaos as Randall had never experienced.

"You have a plan?" Neanderthal asked Randall.

"To the tank!" Randall ordered.

With Jesus' shield around them, they sprinted back towards Carter and his tank, though Carter wasn't around anymore. The swan-like creature, Shwang, was carrying the elderly explorer away from the battle on his back. They were headed towards the hexagonal prism that contained the fabled Stone of Ebiziad. Randall watched as Shwang dropped Carter, who prodded the prism with his cane, prompting a small sliding door to open.

Carter reached inside and pulled a silvery glowing object out.

What happened next was quite remarkable. Swirling storm clouds appeared above the village. A beam of red light burst forth from the sky and engulfed Carter.

Shwang stepped back in alarm as half a dozen star spawn closed in on the pair. The light dimmed and Carter stood staunch in the face of the attack. He tapped the ground with his cane and huge pillars of earth rose up, sending the star spawn tumbling away. Carter pointed his finger towards the star spawn, and incandescent bolts of lightning shot down from the storm, crossing the battlefield in a burning web.

"I'm confident they have this under control," Neanderthal said in awe as he watched the old man use his newfound power.

"The man risks his own destruction to use that power" Jesus murmured.

"I'm sure he knows what he's doing," Randall said, gripping the thick veins on the side of the bio-tank.

"Look at the sky!" Neanderthal shouted as he pointed upwards.

Eyes, in their thousands, pierced the storm and filled every expanse of empty space. The battle had captured the attention of Yog-Sothoth, who now lingered above as a demonic alien overlord.

Randall clambered up and through the hatch first. The inside of the bio-tank was not what he expected. It was a small room devoid of any visible control apparatus. The inside looked like a collection of greenish-grey sinew and veins transporting a clear liquid through the device.

Jesus, then Neanderthal, plopped in behind Randall.

Randall pressed his arms to the front wall of the room, and the insides of the tank squirmed to life. His arms were quickly wrapped to his elbows in stinking sinewy muscle. The feeling was wet and extremely uncomfortable.

Like a sixth sense, Randall could suddenly perceive the entire area around them. He thought about turning the tank, and it spun on the spot. Neanderthal was flung from his feet into the side wall as the device rotated in mid-air.

"Hold onto something!" Randall called as he willed the tank forward.

With a low grumble, the bio-tank moved across the battlefield towards the forest. The star spawn ignored them completely as they zoomed into the inferno consuming the trees.

"Do you know the way?" Neanderthal yelled.

Randall gulped. He had no idea how to find the ruins.

"You won't need to know the way," Jesus stated calmly, sitting on the floor and crossing his legs.

Randall wanted to ask why and then quickly understood. The tanks would've created a wide swathe of destruction as they approached the village. Once they were clear of the inferno, Randall would be able to feel the destruction of the star spawn army's march towards the village through the tank's extra-sensory perception.

They quickly left the fire and battle behind. The chorus of explosions and alien cries didn't carry far into the forest. The tank easily smashed through the fleshy trees, and as Jesus predicted, they came across the tracks the star spawn army had taken to the village.

In the quiet of the dark Randall, at last, took a moment to relax. He hadn't even had the chance to properly comprehend that he was now driving an alien war machine with his mind. With a thought, he spun the main turret three hundred and sixty degrees. War Snail and Tyrannogod had intended on accompanying them to the ruins, though the tank would provide an equally effective tool to assault the star spawn, if it came to that.

Neanderthal leaned against the sinewy walls and closed his eyes. Dirt lined his face and merged into his brown stubble. The soldier had fought valiantly to defend a village of non-human creatures.

"Why did they attack the village?" Randall asked.

Neanderthal rubbed his forehead as he considered his answer. "Well, the most worrying answer is that the star spawn noticed my scouting missions with Tyrannogod and took it as a threat."

"I think it might be something different," Randall offered. "I suspect that the star spawn haven't been able to activate their portal machine yet. There is a good chance they know of the library beneath the village and went in search of information."

Neanderthal shrugged, "Yeah, that could be it."

It made sense to Randall.

Neanderthal rested as Jesus closed his eyes to meditate. They glided through the forest in silence, accompanied only by the occasional shriek of a wailer in the distance.

Randall felt the path travel downhill, and then he sensed something other than trees. The images of buildings appeared like a three-dimensional model in his mind. Arches and ziggurats of green stone glowed in the gloom.

"We're here," Randall murmured. Obeying his commands, the sinewy controls of the tank retreated from his arms and with a clunking *thunk*, the machine lowered to the ground.

Neanderthal groggily pushed the entry hatch open and pulled himself out first. Jesus followed, offering a hand to Randall.

The three men stood before the scattered buildings, in plain sight of any watchers. Yet, there was no movement. The ruins seemed deserted.

"Are we ready?" Neanderthal asked quietly, quickly inspecting his rifle.

Randall nodded, adrenaline and nervous apprehension flooding him.

Neanderthal stepped into the green fog. Randall wished he had a weapon on him. It was foolish for him not to have grabbed anything from the battle site.

The squashed ovals of light flashed high above as the trio stepped silently across open ground. Neanderthal scanned all around, while Jesus loped along with casual grace. Within a minute they came to the teleportation pad Randall had escaped through, now repaired. The roofless pillars of the shrine rose into the mist, looming above them. There was only room for them to use it one at a time. During the previous days, Randall had briefed the others on exactly what he'd seen in the portal room. They all knew the pad would take them to right beside the main device.

Randall laughed at the sudden bizarre thought that he was praying the operating chamber would be empty when the figure most people prayed to was right beside him. Prayer was no good in the Dark World.

"How do we activate it?" Neanderthal asked Randall, shaking him from his thoughts.

Randall had no idea. He knelt down and placed his hands on the cool metallic surface. Much as the tank had reacted to him, the teleporter revved like an engine and spun to life. If their approach had been unnoticed so far, the pillar of light that now shone was guaranteed to give them away.

Click, click, click.

"We have to go now!" Randall urged.

Neanderthal gritted his teeth and stepped into the light. He vanished in a cloud of swirling particles. Randall followed and was engulfed in light before emerging in the tentacle-infested portal chamber.

All hell broke loose.

Bullets flew over the top of Randall's head as Neanderthal fired at the far wall. One of the star spawn, like a grotesque spider, was clambering down towards them. Randall spun on the spot and saw there were two more in the room, running full tilt on all fours towards Neanderthal.

Tentacles clumsily wrapped Randall's ankles, causing him to jump and stamp down aggressively.

"Close your eyes!" Neanderthal yelled, pulling the pin from a flash bang and launching it into the middle of the room.

A blinding light filled the space, disorienting the star spawn. Neanderthal fired deliberate shots into their soft tentacles, causing them to reel back and retreat.

"Whatever you're gonna do, do it now!" he said, exasperated.

Jesus appeared, accidentally knocking Randall to the ground.

"Destroy the teleport pad!" Randall ordered Jesus, who promptly channelled his power into the device. The pillar of light disappeared abruptly with a crack and a fizzle.

Jesus pointed his hands at a star spawn warrior, catching it in mid-air right before its pounce landed on Neanderthal.

"Thanks, Lord," Neanderthal breathed, rolling away.

The star spawn crashed to the ground as another crash tackled Jesus, taking the demi-god by surprise.

Randall saw the star spawn attacking Neanderthal wrap its powerful back tentacles around his rifle and rip it from its sling. Neanderthal drew a long silver hunting knife from his military webbing and dived at the hulking creature, slashing at the tentacle with a focused ferocity.

Jesus held his arms up, generating a pulsing shield as the other star spawn struck at him, pushing him against the cryo-tube-laden far wall. For the first time ever, Randall saw Jesus looking slightly panicked as a series of hisses signalled the activation of the pods. More star spawn were waking up.

The third star spawn clicked angrily and stalked towards Randall, its black eyes piercing him. Its flesh hadn't morphed into bio-armour, evidently not finding him to be a threat.

"I can do this!" Randall's mind screamed as an anthem of motivation.

How had it happened when he was in here last? The star spawn had kind of screamed, the tentacles had retreated and the control apparatus had emerged.

"Blessing of Yog-Sothoth, don't fail me now," Randall murmured as he sucked in a deep breath.

"EEEEEEEEEE!" Randall screamed as high-pitched as he possibly could.

The star spawn paused and observed him curiously. Just as before, the tentacles wrapping his feet retreated into the stone. Jesus used the temporary distraction to send his attacker across the room with a pulsing magical blast. With a righteous fury on his face, he crash tackled the star spawn near Randall.

A stalk of green matter and eyes emerged before Randall, transforming into a computer screen at the top. Eyes all around its rim blinked and watched Randall intently.

Much like it had with the star spawn, the two circular platforms holding the black pincers began spinning faster as they zapped with electricity.

"*Yes!*" Randall thought. The interface was behaving exactly as he remembered. The screen was full of numbers fading in and out.

The green hologram of the Earth engulfed the room, spinning to focus on Sydney, Australia.

Randall poked the screen and it went blank, deleting the previous code. As if his mind was working through his fingers, his reverse-engineered equation appeared piece by piece before him on the screen, melting into the surface.

Neanderthal was violently thrown across the room by the large back tentacles of the star spawn, though Jesus reacted quickly enough to catch him with magic. The tubes on the wall began to open as liquid drained onto the floor.

"The time is now, Randall," Jesus said quietly, using his magic to push another of the star spawn away.

"I'm working on it!" Randall replied. The sweat was pouring from him as the numbers and symbols continued to appear in a steady stream. He heard a click as Neanderthal's rifle jammed, the soldier having managed to retrieve it in the chaos.

Neanderthal swapped the empty magazine out of his rifle and loaded a star spawn with rounds, most of which harmlessly pinged off its armoured surface. Swapping quickly between his rifle, handgun and knife, Neanderthal was doing the best he could to hold them off.

The screen blinked. It was done. The entire equation sat in front of Randall in plain view.

"I want to enter this equation, then have it immediately deleted," Randall thought. He focused all of his concentration on this singular command to the machine.

The black pincers sparked with electricity as the multi-levelled platforms turned even faster.

Jesus shielded Randall and Neanderthal from the electrical bolts arching across the room as the star spawn clicked furiously. They paused in their attack to watch the machine as it activated, all of them summoning their armour plating.

A gale whipped up as wind circled the chamber.

"It's working!" Randall called over the roar of the tornado.

"What happens now?" Neanderthal yelled.

Randall had no idea.

Then, the hologram fizzled away as a small black hole spun to life directly above the pincers. It quickly grew in size, intensifying the wind. It looked just like the one that had taken Randall to the Dark World.

Randall looked towards Jesus and Neanderthal and nodded. This was it. It had to be.

The star spawn understood what was happening and clawed towards the portal. Neanderthal pulled the pin on his last incendiary grenade and launched it at the star spawn, who retreated as fire crossed the floor.

"NOW!" Randall called, running towards the ever-expanding black hole. It had now entirely covered the pincers, becoming a shimmering sphere on the upper platform. Unlike the portal that had taken him here, this one didn't suck anything towards it. It just sat there, an ominous lightless void beckoning him away from the Dark World.

Randall ducked beneath the reaching tentacles of the star spawn and crossed the event horizon.

Daylight, as blinding as staring into the sun, pierced his eyeballs. It was bright, far brighter than he was used to. Gone was the gloom of the Dark World. This was the light of Earth's star.

Randall squinted and wobbled, feeling abnormally heavy. He quickly perceived his location. He recognised Sydney's Circular Quay, or at least, what used to be Circular Quay. It was like a bomb had gone off, shattering the waterfront area.

The sea was churning as unnumbered star spawn breached the surface. And just behind the dreadful aliens was something much worse. Something malevolent.

Standing above the ruined Opera House was a towering monster. There was no mistaking this being. The great old one,

Cthulhu, was awake. His war had begun.

Randall felt the air twist as Neanderthal appeared beside him. The soldier looked at Cthulhu with defiance.

"So, this is our foe," he murmured.

Jesus stepped onto the destruction of Sydney Harbour, and with a small pop, the portal closed behind him.

Jesus shared Neanderthal's look as he stared up at the ancient enemy of the primordials.

"Cthulhu has risen… are you prepared?" Neanderthal asked Jesus.

"I do not know what dark fate awaits me as I face down this ancient demon, but rest assured I will not let this monster claim any part of our world as his own."

"We just need time to gather an army of our own," Randall said.

The armoured hands of the star spawn gripped the ruined concrete around them as the army pulled itself onto land.

"I'll hold back Cthulhu as long as I can. Get away from the front lines of this battle, into the ruins of the city," Jesus ordered and he stepped towards the churning ocean.

"Come on!" Neanderthal yelled.

Randall didn't need to be told twice. He turned and bolted away from the harbour, just behind the Navy SEAL. The battle for Sydney was about to begin, and the prize was planet Earth.

THE STORY WILL CONCLUDE IN:

IN THE SHADOW

OF THE

SUNDERED KING

DID YOU KNOW?

Hello everyone! I hope you enjoyed Randall Dare's adventure in the Dark World. As my series has grown quite dense now, I thought I'd talk about some of the nods to past books in this story.

CONTINUITY

Did you know that this isn't the first appearance of William Eisenhein Carter? Carter's exploits were first mentioned all the way back in book one! When Joshua Dare is first introduced to The Old World, he rummages through a pile of books and comes across one mentioning a voyage to a mysterious plateau in South America and an adventure in Antarctica, the same expeditions Carter tells Randall about. From the third edition onwards, book one also contains a bonus chapter where Carter is mentioned as being in Achilles Aetos' (the werewolf who bit Josh) party in the Egyptian desert. He even gets a line of dialogue.

Then, in book four, Danni Quinn meets Carter's descendant, Ernst, and gets to explore through his great grandfather's treasures while looking for the stolen Necronomicon. This novella also isn't our first encounter with the Lovecraftian deities Yog-Sothoth and Azathot. Of course, I will take this opportunity to acknowledge Howard Phillips Lovecraft, the famous creator of the outer gods and great old ones.

In a 'blink and you'll miss it' moment, in book two: Rise Golden Apollo, when the gods Hecate, Aion and Moros send the injured Apollo out of time, he sees an enormous black cloud pulsing with red lightning. He hears the piping of flutes and the beating of drums in the cosmic dark. This was the series first introduction to the ultimate being Azathot, though you wouldn't have known it at the time. Then, in book four, both Danni Quinn and Joshua Dare are shown the same cloud by Nyarlathotep.

Neanderthal himself has called on Yog-Sothoth before. During the events of the Wendigo Incident, when Josh is at risk of losing to the wendigo, Neanderthal reads from the madman's Necronomicon. He picks a spell at random and wouldn't you know it, the room quickly becomes full of eyes and tentacles. The Wendigo Incident also marks the first appearance of the wailers. The madman in the forest was keeping them in deep pits dug beneath his home, though neither Josh or Neanderthal got to see them.

Lastly, some of the odder creatures in the Village of the Lost come from my own childhood. When I was a kid, I used to draw and draw and draw. Some of the goofy creatures I created were beings like Shwang and War Snail. So when I say it was like Randall Dare had been thrust into the mind of a child, I meant it literally!

TILL NEXT TIME,
JOEL!

THE OLD WORLD SAGA SO FAR...

BOOK ONE: IN THE SHADOW OF MONSTROUS THINGS

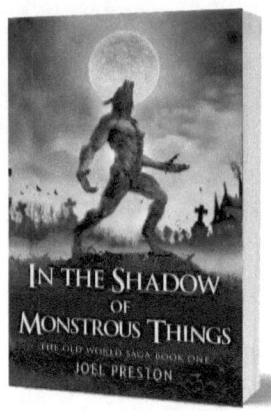

A European holiday takes a sinister turn when Joshua Dare encounters a werewolf. Feeling its bite, Josh escapes, but soon realises that he is now inflicted with an ancient curse. Having to learn how to manage his full moon affliction, Josh is thrust into a world of secret organisations, government operatives and mysterious strangers hunting him. Josh has entered a larger story of gods and monsters, and this is just the beginning...

NOVELLA ONE: THE WENDIGO INCIDENT

Something has angered a supernatural terror in the forests of Minnesota, and the US Government needs help dealing with it. Fortunately, rumours have reached them that the Australians have captured a werewolf. Sometimes to kill a monster, you need a monster of your own. Now, Joshua Dare is off to the USA to assist in bringing down one of Native American folklore's greatest monsters - the wendigo. Other sinister things seem to be happening in that forest too....

Book Two: **RISE GOLDEN APOLLO**

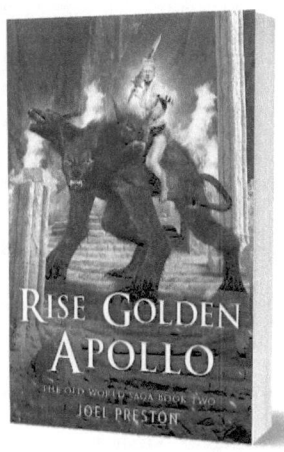

An Australian spy, Melissa Pythia, is searching for a powerful artefact in Rome. More than underworld figures are on her trail as she learns about her connection to a golden sword.

At the same time, in the distant past, the gods of the Underworld are waging war against the angels of Heaven. The surprise attack on the Olympians leaves Apollo lost in time, and only Melissa can bring him back...

Book Three: **IN THE SHADOW OF THE OLD WORLD**

Fearing an information leak and seeking to bolster their alliance with The Old World, the Australian Government has moved Josh Dare to Japan. He is soon tracked down by malevolent supernatural forces who want to exploit his curse. He is the best link to the empty position of Zeus, the vanished god-king. Now, a small team of Australian and US operatives need to work with the gods of old to fulfill an ancient ritual and stop that power falling into the wrong hands.

Novella Two: **EARTH'S MIGHTIEST WARRIOR**

Long ago lived a warrior renowned as the greatest to ever live. Sigurd of the Volsung line has had his story told through the ages, though not all of it. It was thought his tale ended with his death, but then came the war of gods and angels. Now, Sigurd survives as a rat and a champion in Lucifer's new Hell. The tale of Earth's mightiest warrior is only half told. The new legend of Sigurd takes him across the fiery planes of the Underworld, with beings far beyond Norse myth, on his greatest adventure yet.

Book Four: **FALL SILVER ARTEMIS**

Danni Quinn has completed her training and is on her first mission. The goal: finding an artefact of the lost God Zeus. Danni and her boss, the reincarnated Oracle of Delphi, Melissa Pythia, set out to find the Goddess Artemis. Travelling across the scorched plains of Hell they meet the long dead hero, Sigurd the Volsung, who agrees to aide them on their quest. Danni's team heads down a path towards sunken cities and alien horrors. With the help of her former flame, Joshua Dare, and the rest of the AST, Danni will risk everything to complete her mission…

www.ingramcontent.com/pod-product-compliance
Lightning Source LLC
Chambersburg PA
CBHW020524120726
47904CB00003B/961